ALL GIRL

LESBIAN EROTICA BUNDLE

VICTORIA RUSH

COPYRIGHT

All Girl © 2021 Victoria Rush

Cover Design © 2021 PhotoMaras

All Rights Reserved

For the uninhibited...

TURN UP THE HEAT IN YOUR LIFE!

To receive more free books and other steamy stuff, sign up for my newsletter.

Victoria Rush Erotica

VOLUME ONE

THE GIRL NEXT DOOR

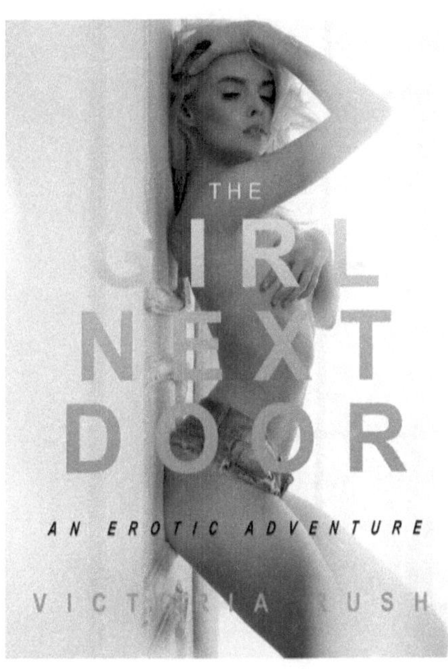

1
———

KEEPING UP WITH THE JONESES

I'd always considered myself a good neighbor. I'd kept my property in good repair, exchanged pleasantries whenever our paths crossed, and tried to respect everyone's personal space. But there's only so much privacy one can maintain when your homes are separated by a modest wooden fence. Especially when you live in a two-story house.

From my master bedroom balcony, I had a commanding view of my fellow residents' backyards. It didn't take long to figure out who lived in each abode, and everybody's predilections. Whether they liked to skinny-dip in their pool, sunbathe in the nude, or cavort in their hot tubs, it was pretty hard to hide from prying eyes.

Not that I made a point of spying on my neighbors. But the ones on my immediate west side were unusually reclusive. I knew they had a single teenage daughter because I'd seen her playing in the backyard when she was younger. But unlike all the other neighbor kids, she hardly ever left the house. She never got on the school bus rounding the neighborhood, and she rarely swam in their large in-ground swimming pool.

On the few occasions that she did venture into the water, it was always in a full-piece swimsuit. I watched her blossom over the years from a skinny pony-tailed girl to a full-figured, voluptuous young woman. With her shapely figure, long blonde hair and full sensuous lips, she looked like a young Marilyn Monroe. The perfect girl next door.

But I couldn't help feel sorry for how she'd been sheltered by her parents. There were no gentleman callers, no prom dates, no giddy sleepovers with her schoolmates. With her home-schooling, who knows what other worldly pleasures she'd been denied? The more often I caught fleeting glimpses of her, the more intrigued I became with her. I'd shamelessly spy through my shutters to catch a glimpse of her patting her wet body dry after a dip in the pool.

Counting the years since she'd fully developed, I figured she was approaching college age. One night, I knew a change was in the wind when I overheard her parents whispering on their back patio.

"We've got to let her go *one* day, Frank," a woman's voice said.

"I know, but college is such a huge step," a middle-aged man replied. "She hasn't been on her own her whole life."

"Abby's a smart girl," the woman said. "We've taught her well. She'll be fine. Besides, she's a grown woman now. If you ever want grandchildren, she'll eventually need to find a mate. Emory's a good Christian college. It won't be that big a leap for her."

"But it's halfway across the country—"

"There comes a time when every young person needs to spread her wings. This is Abby's moment to begin making her own way in the world."

"Miriam—"

"I've been thinking," the woman interrupted. "Summer's almost over. Why don't we take that trip to Europe we've been putting off for so long? We can have some time to ourselves and give Abby a little space to start looking after herself. That way it won't be such a shock when she leaves home."

"How long did you have in mind?"

"Two weeks. Enough time for us to do a little sightseeing and for Abby to get used to being alone."

"What if there's an emergency?"

"Aunt Jenny's only a half-hour away. Plus, Abby's got her driver's license and already knows how to cook and clean up after herself. How much trouble can an eighteen-year-old get into in two weeks on her own? We can call her every day if you're that worried."

The man sighed.

"All right, hon. I suppose we're going to have to let her be on her own one way or the other."

"Good. Because I've already booked the plane tickets for next week."

2

_____

STOLEN GLANCES

In the days leading up to her parents' flight to Europe, all I could think about was Abby. She'd finally be alone, free to express herself and do anything she wanted. At the very least, I hoped she'd spend a little more time in her backyard. A late-summer heat wave had struck the city, and there'd be plenty of opportunities for her to take a refreshing dip in the pool. Maybe she'd been secretly harboring a two-piece swimsuit or — God forbid — planning a skinny-dip after dark. Either way, I'd be glued to my balcony in hopes of stealing another glance at her sweet, nubile body.

But after her parents left, I was disappointed to see her resume her sequestered ways. One day she left the house to pick up groceries and a couple of days later a middle-aged woman I presumed to be her aunt visited for a couple of hours. But during that first week, she ventured into her backyard only a few times to sunbathe in her one-piece suit. By the middle of the vacation fortnight, I began to despair of seeing any part of her beyond her bare legs.

One night as I was getting ready for bed, I noticed her bedroom light was on later than usual. Our windows faced each other on the same side of our house, but she'd always kept her curtains drawn for privacy. Tonight though, I noticed a sliver of light emanating from a crack in the canopy. I crept up to the side of my window and separated my blinds with two fingers, then peered across the narrow laneway.

Abby was sitting at her desk, peering at a computer screen. She was wearing a light nightgown, and I could see the outline of her full breasts from the backlight of the computer through the gauzy material. The screen was flickering with some kind of moving image, but it was hard to make out what she was watching from my distance about twenty feet away. I reached into my nightstand and pulled out a pair of binoculars that I kept on hand for occasional neighbor spying.

Raising the field glasses to my eyes, I gasped when I adjusted the focus and zoomed in on her. The image on the screen was a porno, showing a man and a woman having missionary sex on a bed! I tilted my binoculars down a few inches and saw Abby had her legs spread apart with her hand moving in a strange thrusting motion between her thighs.

She's masturbating while watching the video!

I've never pulled my clothes off my body so quickly in my entire life. I stripped off my jeans and dropped my panties to the floor and immediately began circling my clit. My pussy was already soaked in excitement, as my juices ran down the inside of my legs. I struggled to steady the binoculars with my left hand as I furiously tribbed myself with my other hand.

As Abby watched the video, her mouth parted and I could see a pink flush on her cheeks. Her tits bounced up and down under her skimpy negligee as she rocked gently in her chair, while she thrust her fingers between her legs in rhythm with the lovers on the bed. I was just about to come when the man in the video lifted himself off his lover and stood by the side of the bed while she began to perform fellatio. Suddenly, Abby removed her hands from between her legs and lifted a strange green object in front of her face. It was a large cucumber!

Poor girl, I thought. *She doesn't even have a proper vibrator, having to resort to common household vegetables to get off.*

But what she did next soon made me forget about her deficiency of sex toys. She placed the end of cucumber in her mouth and began sucking on the tip, imitating what the woman was doing in the video. Then she moved her left hand back between her legs and began moving it rapidly up and down. I could see her body shaking in obvious pleasure as she sucked on the green phallus.

This girl is going to make at least one Christian college boy very happy.

The man in the video placed his hands at the side of the woman's head and began deep-throating her. I could see his butt cheeks contracting as he thrust his hips forward, while Abby mimicked his movements with her own rocking action on her chair. Suddenly the man stopped thrusting as he held the woman's head tightly against his stomach.

Abby pulled the cucumber out of her mouth and thrust it between her legs, then arched her back and moaned. I didn't realize that her window also was ajar a few inches, and the sound carried clearly over the small space between our houses. I'd hardly paid any attention to my own pleasure up to that moment, but when I saw her coming, I thrust my fingers into my snatch and gushed all over my hand, biting my lip to stifle my own screams of euphoria.

Abby rested for a minute with the cucumber still embedded in her pussy, then she grabbed the computer mouse and the screen flashed a few times before she settled on a new video. I turned my binoculars back to the monitor and noticed this time the video was of two naked women scissoring on the floor. Abby paused for a moment as I saw her eyes widen and her mouth part in surprise. Then she grabbed the cucumber with two hands and started pumping it into her cunny.

Fuck, that's hot! She likes women! Thank God.

My mind was already racing with thoughts of how I could entice her into my bed. But right now, I needed something in my *own* honeypot. I reached back down into my night table and pulled out my favorite vibrator, then I turned it on maximum and plunged it deep into my snatch. Abby and I were both fucking ourselves watching other women getting off, but suddenly Abby looked up and turned her head in my direction.

Had she noticed the movement in my window? I froze with the vibrator buzzing away in my pussy, suddenly aware that I was standing stark naked in front of my window with the shades half open. As she stared in my direction and squinted her eyebrows trying to detect any sign of intrusion, I suddenly came at the thought of her seeing me. My orgasm consumed me, and I struggled to remain motionless as my upper body quaked and quivered in powerful convulsions. I stared back at her, praying she hadn't noticed me.

When she returned her attention to her screen, I suddenly became aware of the dim glow that was being cast in my own room from my open bathroom door. I quickly walked over to the bathroom and turned off the light, then returned to the edge of the window and peered through the blinds. When I looked back up at Abby's window, she'd pulled her curtains and I could only see the faint shadow of her voluptuous body standing behind the sheers.

Fuck! I cursed.

Whether she'd been distracted by the flickering light in my room or she'd noticed me watching her, was unclear. Either way, I didn't care. I'd finally seen her magnificent body in all its glory, and we'd shared a powerful moment of pleasure together. And now that I knew she was sexually active and attracted to girls, I had other plans. I was already thinking of how I could escalate our secret rendezvous.

3

———

LAYING THE BAIT

I had difficulty sleeping that night thinking about what had happened between me and the girl next door. Beyond my obsessive thoughts of seeing Abby playing with herself, I couldn't help wondering why she'd left her window ajar. Had she just been trying to get some fresh air from the stifling heat of the day? Had she simply forgotten to close her curtains all the way? Or had she left them open *intentionally* hoping I'd see her?

Had she been watching *me* also all these years?

My mind raced with fantasies of fucking this shy vixen. Even though she was all grown up, she'd probably never felt the delicate touch of another man or woman. Her mother was right—Abby needed to find her own way in the world, and soon. College would be crawling with thousands of predatory men trying to take advantage of such a beautiful innocent girl. She needed to be educated in the ways of tender lovemaking before getting a rude awakening.

After watching Abby fuck herself with the huge cucumber, I rushed downstairs to retrieve one from my own fridge. I was startled at first by the feel the cold vegetable in my pussy, but it didn't take long to warm up inside my steaming love tunnel. There was something about the texture and feel of the cucumber that made it feel almost like a real cock. Unlike my vibrator, it had a certain sponginess to it. It had the firmness of a man's hardon, but it was flexible like the real thing. The lack of artificial vibration, far from being a detriment, actually was a welcome change from my oscillating dildo. It felt like a real man inside me—just a better hung one. Maybe Abby wasn't so deprived after all. As I lay on my bed with splayed legs replaying the image of Abby pumping her pussy with the giant legume, I got an idea.

I watched for any sign of movement from Abby the next day, but her curtains remained closed and she didn't venture outside. I still harbored hope that the little glimpse she'd provided me the previous night wasn't just a coincidence. At dusk, I repositioned my bed against the opposite wall so that it was directly facing my window. Then I opened my blinds half way and slid the window open a few inches. I turned on my night table lamp so that it cast a soft glow over the covers. Then I took off all my clothes and lay face up on top of my sheets and closed my eyes.

If Abby happened to glance out her window, she'd see me stark naked, looking like I'd fallen asleep trying to catch a break from the heat. But I had a lot more than just *sleeping* on my mind tonight. I squinted through half-closed eyelids at Abby's window for over an hour but didn't see any sign of movement. It was approaching 10:30 p.m., and I assumed she'd soon be getting ready for bed. Eventually, I saw some flickering light coming from behind her curtains.

No, Abby! Look out your window, not at your computer! I'll give you a much better show than any of those pornos, and it'll be the real thing.

I squeezed my thighs together in frustration, then remembered what had brought her to her window yesterday. I leaned over and turned my night table lamp on and off twice in rapid succession, then I leaned back down. Through the corner of my eye, I could see her shadow moving behind the thin curtains. Then I noticed the corner of the drape open on one side and a dark figure blocking the light from her room. She was looking out her window! I knew she could see me clearly across the laneway in the soft illumination of my bedroom in the pitch dark of night. Now it was just a question of whether I could maintain her interest.

I shifted my position as if I was having a restless dream while keeping one eyelid open just enough to see her outline through the window. She didn't move. But I had to be careful. I didn't want to make it look like I was luring her into some kind of a trap or make her feel uncomfortable. I still wasn't sure that she'd seen me yesterday or that she knew I'd seen her. I needed to maintain the illusion that I was sleeping, or at least that I hadn't noticed her watching me from across the laneway.

I lifted my right hand off the bed and let it flop on my stomach like I was unconscious. Then I began to shift my hips in rhythmic movements as if I was having an erotic dream. It was electrifying to know that Abby was watching my naked body just as I had watched her the previous night. After a few minutes of suggestive hip action, I felt daring enough to begin fondling my tits. I cupped my left breast and began pinching my nipple while continuing to sway my hips. Abby was locked in position by the edge of her window. I knew I had her. Now it was just a matter of pulling her in.

After a few more minutes of squeezing my breasts and writhing suggestively on the sheets, I began to move my left hand down my stomach towards my pussy. I paused for a moment with my fingers on the edge of my pelvic bone while I lifted and swayed my hips. My bare pussy throbbed in anticipation of my touch. The thought of Abby watching me perform my tantalizing tease was intoxicating, and I felt the wetness accumulating on my lips.

I glanced out the corner of my eye and detected some movement of the curtain near the bottom of Abby's window. Her hips were swaying in synchronicity with mine behind the curtain. She was getting just as turned on as I was! I spread my legs further apart and moved my left hand slowly down over my pubis. Trying to play with yourself while pretending to be asleep was more difficult than I thought, and I wasn't sure how much longer Abby would buy the ruse.

But it no longer mattered. As long as I had a captive audience, I intended to make the most of it. I'd give her a show she'd never forget while enjoying something I'd never experienced before. I'd taken this whole spying-on-the-neighbors thing to a whole new level. When I finally touched my clit, I flinched in pleasure. My button was already poking out from under its hood and it was flaming hot. I mixed in the juices from my sopping pussy and circled my nub as I lifted and swayed my hips for my private audience.

I could have come right away, but I wanted to savor the moment and make it last. Plus I had a lot more in mind for the education of my innocent voyeur. I could feel the juices running down my vulva onto my ass, and I moved my other hand between my legs and began to fuck myself with my fingers. My pussy began to make sexy slurping sounds and I moaned loudly as I felt the pleasure rising in my belly.

Suddenly, I heard the sound of Abby's window sliding open as she shifted her weight a few inches away from the edge of her window. She'd obviously heard my muted moans through the glass and wanted a clearer connection. The drapes parted a little further, and I could see the full outline of her hourglass hips against the back-light of her bedroom. Before the curtains closed again to a narrow sliver, I caught a glimpse of a dark patch between her legs.

Of course she'd be unshaven, I thought. *She probably doesn't even know what all the girls are doing these days in terms of intimate grooming.*

Her natural appearance made me even more turned on, and I fucked myself harder as I imagined kissing her furry mound. My orgasm was getting closer, and I began thrashing my hips on my bed while I circled my clit with one hand and fucked myself hard with the other. Abby's curtains parted a little further, and I saw her hand moving between her legs under her thin negligee. That was enough to put me over the edge, and I screamed like a wild animal as I came. I no longer cared if Abby thought I was asleep or not, I just wanted to let the pleasure pour out of me. I heard a little peep emanate from Abby's window and I saw her knees buckle as her chest jerked in rhythmic spasms behind the curtain.

My contractions lasted for almost a full minute as I clamped my hand inside my pussy, giving Abby a full view of my naked body in the throes of ecstasy. After I finally calmed down and stopped moving, I noticed Abby was still standing at the side of her window with the curtains slightly parted.

That's my girl, I thought. *Stay there, baby. Momma's got a lot more where that came from.*

I flipped over, stretching my arms and legs lazily, and lifted my bare ass in her direction.

If you like the front of my body, wait till you see my backside.

I was proud of how I'd maintained my body tone for my age. Regular workouts at the gym and the yoga studio had kept my ass firm and round and tight. I spread my legs slightly to give Abby a glimpse of the dark tunnel between my legs, then I began to raise and lower my ass, beckoning her in. It felt sexy showing her my backside, but from my prone position, I could no longer see what she was doing in her window.

I reached over to my nightstand and tilted my phone up against the front of my clock radio, then twisted it until I could see Abby's reflection on the screen. The dark glass provided a perfect view of the illuminated window across the dark passageway. I wasn't sure if she could see my reflection as well, but it must have been obvious what I was doing, and she didn't flinch away.

Now that I'd reestablished our two-way line of communication, I returned my attention to my aching pussy. I slid my hands under my hips and spread my legs further apart, then placed my fingers under my mound and began fingering myself with both hands. I was still at the height of arousal from my last orgasm and knew it wouldn't be long before I came again. As I began to hump my bed, contracting my buttocks in rhythm with my hands, I heard some moans emanating from Abby's window.

At this point, I had no more interest in carrying on the illusion that I was half asleep. I lifted myself up on all fours and spread my ass cheeks to show Abby my soaking snatch. She had a commanding view of my open pussy and ass, and I leaned my shoulders down on the bed so she could also see my tits hanging between my legs. I reached around with my left hand and plunged my fingers into my cunt while I jilled my clit furiously with my other hand.

I was grunting like a wild animal at the thought of Abby watching me fuck myself from behind. But there was still one thing missing. I reached under my pillow for the cucumber that was still coated with my slippery juices and slammed it into my ass.

I bet this is something you haven't yet seen in one of your pornos!

I looked in the reflection of my phone and noticed that Abby was no longer standing at the edge of her window, hiding behind the curtains. She had pulled them aside and was standing in full view of the open window, with the backlight from her room shining through her flimsy negligee. I could see her full breasts bouncing on her chest as she rubbed her pussy frantically.

She was moaning without abandon now, and I joined her in our shared pleasure. My orgasm hit me without warning, and I couldn't help screaming her name as I gushed onto my hands and clamped down on the cucumber embedded in my ass. Abby screamed out loud too, and the whole neighborhood must have heard our cries of ecstasy as we climaxed in glorious union.

I knew now, that this was going to be the start of a glorious friendship.

4

___

HEAT WAVE

When I woke up the next morning, Abby's curtains had been pulled back and I could clearly see into her room. A small four-poster bed was neatly made up with pink throw cushions and linens. A tall bureau sat next to it with a collection of stuffed animals resting on top. In the far corner, a large pink dollhouse sat unused on the floor. Overhead, a fan with Alice-in-Wonderland leaf-shaped blades whirled quietly on the ceiling. Other than her computer desk and bookcase filled with high school home-study books, it looked like a typical young girl's bedroom frozen in time.

But for most of the morning, there was no sign of Abby. I wasn't sure what to make of the conflicting signals. She'd finally opened a portal to her world, which couldn't have been a coincidence. But why was she being so coy staying hidden? Was she feeling embarrassed about the intimate moment we'd shared the previous night? Had she noticed me watching her in the reflection of my phone on the nightstand? Why would she open her drapes if she didn't want me to see her?

Just before noon, I heard the front door of her house open and close, and I rushed to my living room to peek out the window. She climbed into a Toyota Echo sitting in the driveway, then backed up and turned in the direction of downtown. Was she going to visit her Aunt? Was she heading out to replenish her groceries?

Or was she going to the police station to complain about her peeping Tom neighbor?

For the next couple of hours, I paced my house second-guessing whether I'd pushed the envelope too far. I still wasn't entirely sure she was even of legal age. What if she'd taken a *video* of me? Could that be used to prove that I was some kind of criminal, trying to lure an under-age child into illicit sex? My mind raced with all manner of scary scenarios, with patrol cars screeching into my driveway and burly policemen hauling me off to jail.

After a couple of hours, my heart rate finally returned to normal when I realized the cops would have already arrived at my door if she'd intended to report me. But I knew I had to be far more discreet in my outreach efforts going forward. There could be no more private nude shows, at least until I verified she was eighteen. I used the free time waiting for her to come back to formulate a plan.

I figured it couldn't be easy for her cooking her own meals for the first time in her life. It must be overwhelming having to cook and clean and look after that big house all by herself. I resolved to bring her a ready-made dinner that night. If she was amenable, I'd invite her over to my place, where I could take care of all the details and free her from having to worry about cleaning up. But what kind of food did she like? What does a sheltered home-schooled teenager like for dinner?

After some deliberation, I decided to bake her a chicken casserole. Chicken was pretty safe, and if she didn't accept my invitation, it would be easy for her to simply heat it up in her oven. I could toss a fresh salad as a side, and offer her a glass of wine to help her relax. But not until I verified her age. I probably wasn't the only nosy neighbor checking out the comings and goings in the neighborhood. The last thing I needed was to get either one of us in trouble for underage drinking. Or underage sex.

Jeesh. How could I broach that subject delicately?

I decided to run out to stock up on fresh groceries, and when I returned I noticed Abby's car in her driveway. I hurried inside and rushed upstairs to my bedroom. When I peered out my window, I saw that Abby had closed her drapes again.

Now what? I thought. *Is she having second thoughts about what she'd seen last night? Had she only opened the window to let in a little fresh air from the oppressive heat?*

I walked onto my balcony and peered into Abby's backyard. It was quiet as a mouse. If she planned to retire back into her shell, I had one last chance. There was no harm in being neighborly by offering to share a meal I'd baked. At least this way, I could confront her directly and see if she was as interested as I was in her. For the next hour, I focused on preparing the casserole, while keeping my eyes and ears open for any sign of activity from next door.

Just as I was placing the baking dish in the oven, I heard the distinctive sound of someone diving into a pool. It sounded like it came from Abby's side, and I raced upstairs to peer out my balcony into her yard. When I glanced at the pool, I saw Abby's unmistakable form swimming across her pool.

But this time, she was wearing a skimpy yellow two-piece swimsuit. I watched her tight round bottom wiggling through the water as the yellow shorts clung to the crack in her ass. As she turned her body from side to side, the side of her firm breasts rose tantalizingly above the edge of the water before plunging again below the surface. I was absolutely mesmerized watching her magnificent figure slide through the churning water.

After four or five laps, she stopped at the end of the pool closest to me and lifted her head out of the water, then shook the drops from her hair. She glanced up in my direction and I quickly slunk back behind my bedroom door. I was sure she'd seen me staring at her again, and I cursed myself for being such a pussy. This cat and mouse game, as sexy as it was, was getting tiring.

I went into my bedroom and pulled a racy romance novel out of my nightstand then turned the chair on my balcony towards Abby's house and sat down. If she caught me peering in her direction, I didn't care. I was simply catching some sunshine on a warm day while enjoying a good book. If she chose to run around in a skimpy bikini, that was her business.

When I returned to the balcony, Abby was standing by the side of the pool toweling herself dry. She seemed to linger longer than usual patting her breasts and the area between her legs, and I could have sworn I saw her glance up in my direction again. I tried to hold my gaze on my book, but I wasn't reading a single word. I peered over the top of the paperback, trying to cover as much of my face as I could get away with.

Abby walked over to the side of her pool near her back fence where two chaise lounge chairs rested, and she reclined one of them to a flat position. Then she placed her towel on the cushions and lay down with her backside pointed directly in my direction.

You little tease, I thought.

The ball was now in Abby's court. She was being just as sneaky and calculating as I'd been. Now it was *her* turn to put on a show for me. At first, she simply lay quietly on the lounge, pretending to soak up the sun. But after a few minutes, she began to shimmy her hips in the same manner I had the previous night. I smiled as I parted my legs, my pussy flooding with juices. I suddenly wished that I'd placed some kind of barrier between me and the narrow railing spindles of my balcony to provide more privacy. But I dared not move for fear of missing a single twitch of Abby's exquisite body.

After a few minutes of rolling her hips seductively, she shifted her arms from over her head and rested them at her sides beside her ass. Then she lifted her hips and moved her right hand under her pelvis.

Holy Fuck! I gasped out loud. *She was going to finger herself in plain view, just as I had yesterday!*

There was no longer any doubt that she'd seen me watching her the previous nights. She was going to torment me in exactly the same way I'd done with her. I glanced around at my fellow neighbors' properties to check that we were alone. It was a hot weekday afternoon, and most people had either retreated inside their air-conditioned homes or were lying around their fenced-in pools.

Abby had chosen her lounging position carefully, close to the back fence where no one else could see her besides me. Had she also purchased that skimpy yellow bikini today to drive me even more crazy?

I raised my right leg and bent my knee to provide a modicum of cover, then I unzipped the front of my shorts and thrust my fingers under my panties. As I watched Abby's fingers moving in the tight cleft between her legs, I circled my clit and groaned in delirious pleasure. My shorts already had a giant wet spot creeping down the front of my pant legs, as I dripped like a broken faucet watching her play with herself.

I could see Abby's buttock muscles flexing as she humped the chaise lounge cushion. She was faced away from me, so it was hard to see the expression on her face, but I remembered the sweet look of ecstasy I'd seen two nights ago. I looked in front of her to see if there was any reflective object where she might watch me like I had with her last night, but there was none. Apparently, she was content to give me a one-way show.

But then she turned her head to the side and flitted her eyes in my direction. I could tell that she was trying to disguise the fact that she was peeking at me out the corner of her eyes, and I laughed when I realized how obvious it had been when I tried a similar feint last night. I lowered my book and spread my legs as far as I dared as I rubbed my soaking snatch furiously. We both stared at each other for a moment, then her lips parted and I could hear soft moans wafting up to my balcony. This time I couldn't wait for her. I jerked in my chair and pulled my legs together as I came all over my wet hand in my shorts. I groaned out loud from the pleasure sweeping over me, as I shook and convulsed in my chair.

She must have seen me in the throes of orgasm, because within seconds, she suddenly straightened her legs and pointed her toes, and she clenched her cheeks together as her upper body began to shake. We didn't take our eyes off each other the whole time we both came. The feeling of our first direct visual connection was electrifying, and I spasmed in my chair for almost a full minute as I watched the pretty girl in yellow release her inhibitions for the whole world to see.

Two hours later, I knocked on the front door of Abby's house carrying my ready-made casserole. It took quite a while for her to come to the door, and I began to worry that I'd scared her away. If I were in her shoes, I'd be a little nervous too about making direct contact with someone I'd shared such an intimate, but heretofore remote, relationship.

Maybe her parents told her not to open the door for strangers, I thought. *Come on, Abby. You can do this. I won't bite.*

About sixty seconds later, I heard some footsteps approaching the door from the other side, then I saw the view hole flicker as she looked through the spyglass. She hesitated for a moment, then swung the door open.

"Hi," I said. "I'm Jade, your next-door neighbor."

Abby's pupils dilated as big as saucers. Whether it was from excitement or nervousness, I couldn't be sure.

"Yes," she said. "I recognize you. I've seen you...*around.*"

"I hope you don't mind this little intrusion. But I saw your parents leave for a trip a few days ago and noticed that you were all alone. I thought I'd be a good neighbor and bring you a little gift."

I held the covered baking dish in my outstretched arms.

"That's very thoughtful," Abby said. "What is it?"

"It's a little casserole I threw together. It's already cooked. You just need to put it in the oven for thirty minutes to warm it up."

Abby reached out and accepted the dish, then we paused awkwardly for a moment on the doorstep.

"If you'd like, we could share it together," I said. "If you want to come over to my place, I could throw together a nice side salad and we could get to know each other a little better. We've been neighbors for quite a while, and I heard rumors that you'll be heading off to college soon. I'd love to hear about your plans."

Abby hesitated as her eyes fluttered considering the offer. She must have known I had other designs, beyond sharing a meal together.

"Um, okay," she finally said. "When's a good time?"

"How about seven?" I said, trying not to betray the rush of excitement coursing through my body.

"Okay, I'll see you then."

Abby smiled at me, then she closed the door. I practically skipped back to my place with thoughts of what lay ahead that evening.

5

———

THE SWEETEST WINE

For the next two hours, I busied myself preparing for Abby's visit. Fortunately, I'd replenished my fridge earlier in the day and had most of the cooking already done. Now it was just a matter of cleaning up the house and getting myself ready. I washed the sheets and placed some extra cushions on the bed, then cleaned the washroom and hung some fresh towels. I wasn't sure if Abby would make it this far, but I wanted to make everything as welcoming as possible if she did.

Then I had a long shower, dried my hair, and put on some skinny jeans and a silk blouse. I knew I was overdressed for a casual dinner, especially on such a hot day, but I wanted to highlight my best assets in hope of attracting Abby's attention. I considered going braless, but at the last minute erred on the side of prudence over provocation. I didn't want to be too obvious or make Abby feel like I was coming on too strong.

When my doorbell rang at seven that evening, I rushed to the door and took a deep breath before swinging it open. Abby looked more beautiful than ever in matching pastel shorts and blouse, with tasteful leather sandals. Her shimmering blond hair was freshly washed, and she'd applied some light lipstick and mascara that highlighted her natural beauty. My eyes lit up as she stood on the doorstep holding a beautiful bouquet of long-stemmed tulips.

"Abby," I said. "Come in. You look...*lovely*...this evening."

Abby stepped over the threshold and presented the flowers to me.

"Thank you, they're gorgeous. How did you know tulips were my favorite?"

"I didn't, but they're my favorite too. I thought I should bring something..."

I took the flowers from Abby's hands and motioned toward the other end of the house.

"Come to the kitchen while I place them in a vase. Are you hungry?"

"Yes, definitely," Abby said, smiling at me softly. "It's been a while since I've had a good home-cooked meal."

I led Abby into my kitchen and filled a tall vase with water.

"Where did your folks go for vacation?" I asked.

"France, mostly. They were going to spend a week in Paris, then a few days on the Mediterranean coast before taking the train to England and flying back from London."

"How lovely. I hear the French Riviera is beautiful at this time of year. May I ask why you didn't join them? It would have been a perfect going-away gift."

Abby shook her head and shrugged her shoulders.

"They didn't ask. Maybe they just wanted a little alone time. I've been a bit of a handful all these years, with the home schooling and everything. This is the first time any of us have had a real break from one another. Maybe they wanted to make sure I could look after myself before sending me off to college."

I nodded my head as I sprinkled some flower food into the vase.

"College is a big step, especially for someone who hasn't had any prior public education. Are you excited?"

"I have to admit I'm a little scared *and* excited."

Abby watched me for a moment as I clipped the flower stems and arranged them in the vase.

"Do you mind my asking how you knew my parents were going away?" she asked.

I stopped for a moment and looked up.

"Yes, I guess that was a little forward of me. I actually overheard them talking one night on your patio by the pool. Voices carry pretty easily up to my balcony on a quiet night."

"Is that how you knew my name too?"

I placed the vase in the middle of my dining room table then looked up at Abby.

"Yes, sorry if I've been such a nosy neighbor. But it was nice to put some names behind the familiar faces. We've lived next door to one another for so long and never been formally introduced."

Abby frowned as she shifted position uncomfortably.

"My parents are a little overprotective of me. I think it was their religious upbringing. Not wanting me to have any unholy influences, and all that."

"Well there's a lot of *sinful* activity out there," I said, smiling at Abby. I placed a head of lettuce on the cutting board in the middle of my kitchen island and began chopping it into little pieces. "Is that why you so rarely ventured out of the house also?"

"You mean into our backyard, using the pool?" Abby said.

"Among other things."

"After I started developing, they didn't want me exposing my body. When they bought the house, it came with the pool. But they thought I'd be desecrating myself if I exposed too much of my body to strangers."

I shook my head as I sprinkled the lettuce leaves into a salad bowl.

"It's a shame, because you have such a lovely figure. I don't see any harm in displaying your God-given features, if you do it in a tasteful way. I was glad to see you sharing a bit more of yourself by the pool yesterday."

Abby looked away from me and blushed.

"Did you like the new swimsuit?"

"Oh, yes," I said, pulling a large cucumber out of the fridge and plopping it on the cutting board. "I enjoyed it very much. You looked absolutely ravishing in it."

Abby blushed a deeper shade of crimson and turned her body to look through my kitchen window into my backyard.

"You have a lovely home. I see you have a pool also. Do you use it very often?"

Watching Abby stand by the window made me think she'd stolen just as many glances of me swimming half-naked in my pool as I had of her.

"As often as I can. Especially in this summer weather. It's a great way to cool off from the heat." I grabbed a large paring knife and began slicing the cucumber into thin slices. "I especially enjoy swimming in the nude after dark. The water feels magnificent on my naked skin."

Abby shifted uncomfortably as she glanced toward her own backyard.

"That sounds like fun, but my parents would kill me if they ever caught me doing that."

My pussy began to moisten at the thought of watching Abby's naked body snaking through the water.

"You've still got a few days before they return. You should try it. It's very invigorating."

"What about the neighbors? There's not much...*privacy*...with us all huddled so close together."

I smiled at Abby's double entendre. I was beginning to enjoy our little game of verbal brinkmanship.

"If you do it quietly with the lights off, no one will notice. Except maybe the ones who've been watching you ever since you've grown up."

Abby turned around when she heard me pull the casserole out of the oven.

"The dinner smells delicious. Thanks for having me over."

"It's been a pleasure getting to know you, Abby," I said. "Please, have a seat." I uncorked a bottle of wine and paused as I held the open bottle over her goblet. "Are you old enough to drink?"

"I just turned eighteen last month."

"Well we'd better start getting you acclimated," I said, breathing a huge sigh of relief. "God knows, there's going to be plenty of spirits flowing once you get to college."

For the next hour or so, Abby and I made small talk over dinner, talking about her course of study and plans after college. Neither of us broached the subject of what we'd seen and done over the last couple of days, but by her second glass of wine Abby had loosened up and begun to talk about dating. When I started clearing the table and placing the dishes in the sink, she offered to help clean up.

"How about if I do the washing and you help me dry?" I said, handing her a dish towel.

As I filled the sink and leaned over to pour some soap in the water, I caught Abby stealing a glance at my ass.

"So you like boys, then?" I asked.

"I suppose so, but my parents haven't let me go on any dates yet. I'm not sure I'm ready though."

"Really?" I said, passing her the wet casserole dish. "You're eighteen, in the prime of your life, and just about to head off to a place that will be teeming with eligible bachelors. What's your hesitation?"

"I don't know," she said, rubbing the inside of the baking dish gently with her towel. "Lately, I've been finding myself more attracted to...*women*. I'm beginning to wonder if I'm—"

I turned around to face Abby and gently took the casserole dish from her hands and placed it on the counter.

"Abby, you're a smart, beautiful, sexy young woman. Anyone will be lucky to share your love. You'll know when the moment comes what the right decision is..."

I leaned toward Abby's face and hesitated as we peered into each other's eyes. Abby closed the distance and placed her lips softly against mine. Our hips moved together, and I placed my arms around her back and pulled her closer. My mind began spinning as we both moaned in each other's mouths.

I wanted to fuck her right then and there, and it was tempting not to lift her up onto my kitchen counter and pull off her shorts. But I glanced through my kitchen window and realized that we were far too exposed to prying eyes.

"Let's go somewhere where we have more privacy," I said.

I took her by the hand and led her upstairs to my bedroom, then gently lay her down on top of my comforter. I kneeled down beside her and propped myself over her body as I drew my right thigh up between her legs and pressed it against her warm pussy. Abby took in a sudden breath of air, and we gazed into each other's eyes as I lowered my face onto hers. As we kissed passionately, I pressed my mound into the soft flesh between her legs. Abby moaned into my mouth, and her breathing became ragged.

After a few minutes, I lifted myself up and began unbuttoning her shorts, but Abby placed her hand over mine to stop me. I feared that she might be having second thoughts, but then she leaned forward and glanced out my bedroom window.

"Do you mind if I close your blinds?" she said. "I know my parents are away, but it'll make me feel more secure. You never know who else might be watching from a distance."

I smiled and nodded knowingly.

"Of course," I said. "This time, there'll be no one but the two of us."

Abby got up off the bed and walked to the window, then turned the shutter handle to close the blinds tightly. When she walked back toward me, I stood up and blocked her before she reached the bed. Then I looked into her eyes and began unbuttoning her blouse. She looked straight back at me as I separated her blouse and peered at her breasts. She was wearing an old-school brassiere that pulled her breasts tightly together, and I stared at the cleft produced by her large bosom. I reached around her back with two hands and unclasped the latch of the bra, then I raised it and gasped.

Abby had the most beautiful breasts I'd ever seen on the female form. Full and plump, they were perfectly round and firm, sitting high on her chest. If I didn't know better, I might have thought they were surgically enhanced, but of course she was far too young and sheltered to have gotten anywhere near a plastic surgeon. Her areolas were small and dark, with thick nipples protruding almost a full inch off her chest. I cupped her tits with both hands then buried my face shamelessly between her magnificent mountains.

When I lifted my head, I sucked gently on each of her erect nipples. Abby placed her hands behind my head and moaned softly as I licked and stimulated her sensitive teats. I wanted to feast on her like a suckling baby, but the throbbing clit in my wet pants reminded me there was much more to enjoy. After a few minutes of kneading, suckling, and playing with her melons, I finally pulled myself away and kissed her on her lips.

"You're exquisite," I said, looking into her eyes.

"Jade," Abby panted. "Take me. I've been waiting for this for so long."

I pulled Abby's blouse off behind her back, then lifted her bra over her shoulders and threw it softly on the edge of the bed. Then I unbuttoned the front of her shorts and pulled them over her round hips and let them fall to the floor. I was surprised to see her wearing plain white granny-panties that extended almost up to her belly-button.

Jesus, I thought. *I'm going to have to take this girl to the mall to get her properly outfitted for college. This is no way to present herself among trendy university students.*

I placed my fingers under her waistband and slowly pulled her panties down over her stomach. When the band got half way down her abdomen, a tuft of light brown hair puffed out, forming a perfect triangle in the cleft between her legs.

She really hasn't been touched down here at all, I thought.

My mouth watered at the thought of feeling her downy pubic hair against my face.

Abby's legs quivered as I pulled her panties over his hips and lowered them to the floor. I kneeled down in front of her and untied her sandals, as I rolled my head softly against her bush. I could hear Abby panting above me, and I smiled in the knowledge that she was enjoying being touched by another woman for the first time.

When I finished untying her sandals, I placed my arms around her thighs and kissed her on her mound. I breathed in the fresh sweet scent of her pubic hair and closed my eyes. There was something about her natural beauty that was driving me absolutely crazy. As I kissed and nuzzled her soft muff, I raised my hands and cupped her ass.

"God," I muttered audibly, when I felt her firm round cheeks.

Her ass was even more perfect than her tits, if that were even possible. I desperately needed to see her full body in all its naked glory. I stood up and took a step back to look at Abby. She stood with her hands beside her hips, her tummy shaking in anticipation and excitement.

"You're stunning, Abby," I said, taking a long pause to soak up every curve and valley of her magnificent figure. "You're even more beautiful than I imagined."

Abby stepped forward and began clumsily unclasping the buttons on my silk blouse, then I took a step back and motioned for her to stop. I slowly unfastened the buttons myself, taking my time to sexily remove every stitch of my clothes while her eyes grew wider and wider and her stomach fluttered in obvious excitement. When we were both finally naked, we took a moment to appraise other's bodies, then we pressed our bodies together and began kissing passionately.

Abby was a clumsy kisser, unsure what to do with her tongue, and I slowed her down to teach her the proper technique. I placed my hands gently on the sides of her cheeks and began by softly kissing the sides of her lips. I nibbled her lower lip for a few seconds, coating it with my saliva, before inserting my tongue gently into her mouth and swirling it softly inside her. Then I placed my hands beside her head and pulled her into me, turning my face and head to probe her sweet, pliant mouth. As we rubbed our tits and pussies together, Abby's breathing grew heavier and heavier.

I desperately wanted to thrust my fingers into her box and feel her wetness in my hand and give her her first real live orgasm. But I kept reminding myself this was her first time with another lover and that she deserved a tender and measured first experience. After five minutes of passionate kissing, I separated myself again and grabbed Abby's hand and led her to the bed.

I lowered her softly onto the covers, then lay beside her on the bed. We turned and pressed our breasts together and kissed gently for the longest time. I just wanted to feel her delicate skin against mine and breathe in her sweet aroma. My mind spun in a drunken stupor, I was so elated to be finally holding her in my arms.

But there was so much more I wanted to do with her, and before long we separated again and I slowly began kissing my way down the front of her belly. I could feel Abby's stomach shaking the closer I got to her honeypot, but when I reached her mound, I stopped and kissed her soft muff for several seconds. It had been so long since I'd seen or touched a full and natural pubic patch, I reveled in the softness of her downy fur.

Abby twisted and raised her hips, begging me to go lower, and I gently spread her legs apart. I could smell the sweet aroma from her cunny and knew that she wanted me to touch her there. But I began by kissing the insides of her thigh, tantalizingly edging my way up toward her steaming kitty. I wanted to take me time and give Abby the most amazing sexual experience of her life.

When I finally reached her apex, her thighs were already coated in her juices. I placed two fingers over her opening and ran them along the sides of her slippery labia. Abby had a beautiful pussy, with full and plump outer lips framing tight, symmetrical inner lips. Everything about her was like she'd been molded by God himself to create the perfect female form.

Abby whimpered as I played with the outer edges of her flower, then I slowly inserted two fingers into her hole. She grasped my fingers tightly as I pressed them into her, then I began to slowly finger-fuck her as I watched her head roll from side to side in delirious pleasure. I couldn't believe that I actually had my hand inside this gorgeous angel, giving her a pleasure she'd never yet experienced. How lucky was I to be the first one to touch her virgin garden?

Abby began rolling and thrusting her hips more vigorously, and I began to fear she might come before I had a chance to taste her nectar. I lowered my head between her legs and placed my mouth over her throbbing clit, then I sucked her nub between my lips. Abby gasped and raised her hips off the bed, pushing her pussy harder into my face. It felt glorious to finally feel her in my mouth, and I danced my tongue over her clit as I listened to her squealing in unbridled pleasure.

"Yes!" she moaned. "Suck me, Jade. Please suck me. I want to come in your mouth."

I almost came myself when I heard her mention my name, and I clamped my thighs together, trying to give my aching clit some direct stimulation. I could feel Abby's clit hardening in my mouth as her hips thrashed and pressed against my face. I knew she was close when her whimpers turned to squeals, and I curled my fingers toward me, stimulating her G-spot. Suddenly, she lifted her hips off the bed and grasped the side of my head with two hands and squeezed my ears tightly.

"Jade!" she screamed. "I'm coming! God, I'm coming!"

With one final guttural groan, she paused and held my head between her legs as she jerked and spasmed against my drenched face. I could feel the inside of her pussy clamping down on my fingers in rhythmic contractions, as I cradled her softly, savoring every pulse and squirt of her quivering body.

6

———————

TWO BECOME ONE

Abby and I lay quietly on my covers after she came, kissing and caressing each other, as her breathing slowly returned to normal. I ran my hand over her torso, marveling at the size and firmness of her breasts. Even lying down, they pointed high and proud on her chest, like the twin pyramids of Giza. I cupped and squeezed and pinched them, like a child with playdough.

"Are you sure you these things aren't surgically enhanced?" I said, pinching my eyebrows in amazement.

"Are you kidding? My parents would never let me debase what God gave me."

"Well thank you, God, for bestowing this beauty with such perfect and natural gifts. You're really a work of art."

I traced my hand further down her belly and ran my fingers through her soft pubic patch.

"I love your muff, too. It's so soft and...*pure*."

Abby looked between my legs then placed her hand gently on my mound.

"Really? I noticed most of the girls in the videos are shaved like you. You're so smooth—there's no stubble like when I shave my underarms."

I smiled at Abby's delightful innocence.

"I used to have it waxed off, but a few months ago I chose to have all my pubic hair removed with laser treatment. Let's hope the trend with intimate landscaping doesn't change anytime soon, because there's no going back for me."

Abby caressed my mound softly with her hand, then pushed her fingers lower between my legs.

"I like it," she said. "I can feel *all* of you."

I watched Abby's eyes widen as she ran her hands over my bare vulva.

"You know I spied on you a couple of nights ago watching those videos. It was super-hot. Did you leave your drapes and window open on purpose?"

Abby lowered her gaze shyly as she caressed my inner thighs softly.

"Yes. I was kind of hoping you'd notice me. I've been spying on you for years. Watching you get dressed in the morning, sleeping at night..."

I placed my hand under Abby's chin and lifted her face so I could peer in her eyes.

"Is that what you were doing *last* night too?"

"Yes," she sighed. "You were so beautiful and sexy, I couldn't take my eyes off you."

"Did you like the little show I put on for you?"

"Yes. You were very naughty."

"Apparently, we both have a certain affinity for long green vegetables."

Abby blushed, then pressed her tits against me. Her hand circled over the back of my ass as her fingers probed between my legs.

"What can I do for *you* now?" she said. "I want to give you the same kind of pleasure you just gave me."

"Well actually," I said, lifting myself up off the bed. "I had a little something in mind that I think we might *both* enjoy."

I slithered down toward the other end of the bed and positioned myself between Abby's legs.

"No fair!" Abby said, trying to raise herself up. "It's *your* turn. Shouldn't I be the one on top this time?"

I pressed Abby back down onto the bed and smiled.

"There's a lot of ways to have sex besides the missionary position, young lady. Remember that video you were watching the other night? How would you like to try that?"

Abby began to roll and lift her hips seductively.

"Mmm—yes, please. I want to feel you. I want to feel you...*fucking* me."

I raised my eyebrows, then a wide grin stretched across my face.

"You're so naughty. I *like* a naughty girl."

"Show me how you do it, Mommy," Abby said, continuing the role play. "Show this innocent church girl the ways of the world."

"Fuck, yes," I growled.

I pulled her hips toward me and scissored my legs under and around her midsection. When our pussies touched, we were both sopping wet, and I could feel the heat radiating from Abby's oven. She moaned loudly when our clits connected.

"Oh, Abby, I've dreamed of doing this to you for so long. Let Momma cum all over your sweet cunny."

I got up on my knees and pushed my steaming pussy against Abby's hairy snatch and began grinding our hips together.

"Fuck," Abby panted. "That feels so good. Fuck my cunt with your beautiful bald pussy!"

I couldn't believe Abby was talking dirty to me, which turned me on even more. I lifted her right leg off the bed and placed it between my tits as I humped my pussy between her legs. I could feel her wetness coating both of our thighs and our pussies made sexy squishing sounds as our labia rubbed together. Abby's tits shook like two huge Jello molds as she looked between her legs watching me fuck her.

"God, yes!" she panted. "Fuck me, Jade. I want to watch you come like you did for me. I love you."

When Abby said those words, I felt a surge of energy through my body and my pussy tingled in excitement. I pushed my mound hard against hers and wrapped my arms around her extended leg on my chest.

"Abby!" I said, looking straight into her eyes. "I'm going to come baby. I'm going to come all over your sweet virgin cunny."

My climax poured over me like a tidal wave. I pulled Abby's leg hard against my chest and squirted my love juices into her gaping hole.

"Fuck," I screamed. "I'm cumming, Abby! I feel you between my legs. Come with me!"

Abby suddenly opened her mouth like she was gagging, as a deep red flush swept over her chest above her tits.

"Yes," she screamed. "Feel me, Jade! I'm cumming with you. Ohhh, yesssss!"

Abby grabbed my hips and pulled me toward her as we thrashed and ground our pussies together, screaming and panting in ecstatic union. I could feel Abby's fingers digging into the sides of my buttocks as her hips jerked and spasmed in concert with mine. All the while, we never took our eyes off one another. When we finally stopped coming, I held Abby's leg tightly against my chest for another minute as I savored the feeling of our wetness comingling between our joined pussies. Then I collapsed onto the bed beside her and exhaled deeply.

"That was incredible!" Abby panted. "I feel blessed that you're my first."

I turned my body toward Abby and kissed her gently on her lips.

"I'm the lucky one. You're an angel sent down from above. I've never felt—"

I stopped myself before I said something I'd regret. Abby was just starting out in her voyage of exploration, and she was just about to head off for college. It was unfair of me to harbor any expectations beyond our little fling.

"You mean..." Abby said. "You feel it too? Do you—"

I placed my finger over Abby's lips, then I pushed myself back so I could look at her directly.

"You've got your whole life ahead of you, Abby. I'm almost old enough to be your mother. You deserve to experience all the wonders of youth and explore your sensuality with other young people. Some day, long after you've graduated and found your footing in the world, you'll find your soulmate. We'll always have a special connection, and I'll always be your friend, forever."

Two streams poured down Abby's cheeks as her face contorted in pain.

"Does this mean we can't be...*lovers* any longer?"

I pulled Abby toward me and hugged her close to my body.

"We'll always have this special bond, Abby. But I want you to be free to fall in love with other people, to find that special someone you'll be perfectly yoked with. Right now, I think it's mostly the hormones talking."

"What do you mean?"

"Well, when two people make love and have an orgasm together, there's some special hormones that are released that causes them to have certain feelings for one another. It's called the love hormone—oxytocin. Nature, or God, provided us with this so that we'd be more likely to stay together and raise the children that often come after coupling, to ensure a more successful family unit."

"But...we're women. We can't have children this way."

"It's the same hormone, no matter who you're with. And it's a very powerful hormone, like a drug. You'll find it has a similar effect with other people you're attracted to. Don't rush into love—let it find you."

Abby snuggled closer to me and kissed my neck.

"Well whatever those hormones do, I like it. If we can't be lovers, can we at least be *friends with benefits* a little longer?"

I pushed Abby away from me and opened my eyes in mock surprise.

"So that's it? You're going to dump me just like that? Wham, bam, thank you ma'am?"

Abby looked at me coyly and traced a circle around my nipples with her fingers.

"Not exactly. I was hoping we could do a little more whamming and bamming, at least before I go off to college. I'm guessing there's a few more things you can still teach me..."

I flipped Abby over onto her back and pulled myself on top of her.

"You're damn right there is. In fact, I did have something else in mind if you're not too tired and already spent."

"Are you kidding? I'm eighteen! I can come all night with you if you'll let me."

"All right then," I said, getting up off the bed. "You just wait here and keep that pretty little pussy of yours warmed up for me. I've got a little surprise for you."

I hurried downstairs and ran into the kitchen and flung open the fridge. Then I opened the crisper and looked at the special collection of cucumbers I'd purchased at the grocery store earlier today. I picked out the longest and thickest one and bent it gently between my two hands.

This one will do just fine, I thought.

I ran back upstairs holding it behind my back and skipped into my bedroom like a kid on Christmas, stopping a few feet from the bed with a huge Cheshire grin on my face.

"What?" Abby said, a big smile spreading on her face. "What are you hiding behind your back?"

I slowly pulled my arm around in front of me and held the giant cucumber up triumphantly in front of me.

Abby looked at me teasingly and shook her head.

"But we've both already tried that. I thought you were going to teach me something new!"

"Oh, but there's so many ways we can use a big dildo like this," I said, crawling onto the bed between Abby's legs. Let Mommy show you how else one can savor fresh cucumber."

I placed the sprout against the inside of Abby's thigh, and she flinched from the cold texture on her warm skin. Then I slowly slid it up the inside of her thigh until it pressed against her pussy. She gasped when it touched her, and I began to slide it up and down over her wet slit.

"That feels good," Abby purred.

"It feels even better when it's *inside*," I said. "But you already knew that. This is what I mean about experimenting with other people. You really won't know for sure if you just like women until you've felt a man's throbbing cock inside you."

Abby looked up at me, surprised.

"So you don't just like girls?" she said.

"I consider myself *pansexual*," I said. "I like to have sex with the right person in the moment. But I have to admit, I do have a special fondness for women..."

I thrust the tip of the cucumber into Abby's hole and she took a sudden intake of breath.

"Yeah?" I teased. "You like that? There's more where that came from."

As I pushed the cucumber further inside her, I watched it stretch and push her labia apart the further it went.

"Uhnnn," Abby groaned. "Yes, Jade. Fuck me. Fuck me with your big cock."

I began to pump the cucumber in and out of her as I watched her head roll from side to side in pleasure. She thrust her hips in a matching humping action as she fucked and squeezed it in her tight box.

Damn, I thought. *This girl is going to make one hung dude very happy some day. But right now—she's all mine.*

"Deeper," Abby panted. "Fuck me deeper with your big cock, Jade."

I already had about seven or eight inches buried inside her and could feel the end of it pushing up against some resistance.

"It won't go any deeper," I said. "I don't want to hurt you."

Abby tilted her head up and peered at me holding the other end of the vegetable.

"You've only got it half way inside me," she said, teasingly. "It seems a shame to waste so much of it."

I smiled at Abby knowing we had the same idea.

"You're reading my mind, girl. I had no intention of wasting the other half."

I lay down on the bed and spread my legs facing Abby, then I slithered my pussy towards hers and inserted the other end of the cucumber into my slit. As I pushed myself toward her, I could feel the cucumber pushing deeper inside me. Abby groaned as she felt the pressure of it pushing inside her from my movement.

"God, yes!" she panted. "Fuck me, Jade. Fuck me with your big green cock."

I continued twisting and pushing the cucumber inside me until it filled me up. When our pussies finally touched, Abby and I both moaned, then we began rocking our hips together as we fucked the big dildo from opposite ends.

"Ohhh, Uhnnn," Abby groaned, as I clamped down on the dildo and thrust it inside her pussy.

We alternated squeezing and releasing the cucumber within each of our pussies, exchanging the feeling of being fucked and fucking our partner. This was something I'd never experienced before, and I closed my eyes focusing on the incredible sound and feel of the giant cock sliding in and out of our pussies as we ground our clits against one another. Within a few minutes, I felt that familiar sensation rising within me and knew I couldn't hold out much longer.

"Baby," I called out to Jade. "I'm going to come again. Let me feel you gush all over my cunt as we come together. Are you ready?"

"Yes," Abby panted. "I'm going to come all over you. Fuck me hard!"

I sat up and placed my hands beside Abby's hips, pulling her toward me in rhythmic movements as I thrust the cucumber deeper inside her. It was an incredible sight watching the thick green phallus going in and out of her splayed pussy as I fucked her like a man. As I felt my orgasm take hold of me, I squeezed Abby's buttocks and pulled her crotch hard against mine.

"Come for me, baby," I cried. "I'm going to come inside you now. Feel me, Abby," I yelled. "I'm *cumming*!

Abby and I both screamed each other's names as we gushed all over the slick cucumber embedded deep within our pussies. I could feel the walls of my pussy contracting as it gripped the fleshy dildo, and my clit twitched against the hard, cool skin of the vegetable. It was the most incredible feeling coming together with Abby, joined as we were with the juicy object between us.

We shook and panted and whimpered for several seconds, as we climaxed together. When we both came down from our highs, I pulled the wand out of our pussies and lay down beside Abby at the head of the bed. I placed the slippery cucumber between our tits and slid it sexily between our breasts, then I sucked on the end that had been in Abby's pussy.

"Mmmm," I said, looking teasingly into her eyes. I much prefer my cucumbers this way than in a salad."

F or the rest of the week, Abby and I played and made love with each other, trying our best to stay out of the public eye. I was mindful that her parents would be returning from vacation soon, and I didn't want any nosy neighbors spilling our little secret. We pulled the blinds shut then slept together, ate together, giggled together, and bathed together. And we fucked each other deliriously, right up until the last moment.

After her parents returned, we continued our remote affair through our adjoining windows at night, with nobody the wiser. On the day Abby left for college, she snuck over to my place and gave me one last, long lingering kiss. Then I didn't hear from her again until she returned home for the Christmas holidays. Although I missed our secret trysts, I smiled whenever I thought of her, knowing that she'd finally found her independence.

VOLUME TWO

GIRL'S CAMP

1

───────

FALLING FOR THE GIRL

I woke to the sound of my phone rattling on the nightstand. I ignored it for a few seconds, then buried my head under my pillow, squeezing the sides trying to muffle the noise. For the last week or so, I'd had more trouble than usual getting my day started. After the girl next door had gone off to college, I felt hopelessly alone and depressed. Even though our affair only lasted a couple of weeks, it had injected an exciting spark into my love life that had been missing for far too long. Now I was all alone again, with only my freelance graphic design job giving me any reason to get out of bed in the morning.

After a few minutes, the phone started buzzing again, and I rolled over to glance at the screen. It was an incoming call from my best friend, Hannah. Normally, she texted me at this time of the day, so it must have been important. I reached over and tapped the speaker button, then flopped back down on the bed.

"Hello?" I said, groggily.

"Are you *still* not up?" Hannah said. "I'm getting worried about you, girl. You haven't set foot out of your place for over two weeks."

"Welcome to the life of a lonely freelance artist. Sometimes I wonder if it was such a good idea quitting the firm. At least you see some familiar faces every day."

"You haven't been answering my texts lately."

"I've been...*busy*."

"Sleeping in and feeling sorry for yourself?"

I paused, thinking how best to respond. I hadn't told Hannah about my recent fling with the girl next door.

"Something like that."

"Listen," she said. "I've been thinking. Summer's almost over. We need to get you out of the house and get your circulation pumping again. Me and some of the girls from the office were thinking of taking a camping trip."

"What, to Yosemite again?"

"Even better. *Canada*. Lilly knows a quiet place way up north that's hardly been touched by human civilization. We can go full-on commando. Portage in by canoe, catch our own fish, go skinny dipping—the whole nine yards. It'll be good for you to get away for a while. Just you and me and four other girls."

The idea of swimming in the nude with people I knew made me feel a bit uncomfortable. I still hadn't come out with Hannah or anyone else about my recent lesbian dalliances.

"Skinny dipping? Won't it be *cold* up there? That doesn't sound like my idea of relaxing."

"The lakes are small and shallow, not like Lake Michigan. They get super-warm this time of the year. Plus, they're crystal clear and utterly pristine. Lilly says you can actually *drink* from them. When was the last time you felt comfortable doing that?"

I glanced out my window toward Abby's house and sighed.

"I don't know, Han..."

"Well I'm not letting you off the hook this time," Hannah said. "We've already booked the tickets. We fly into Toronto Wednesday morning, drive a rental car north for a few hours, then arrive back home middle of next week. Your freelance business can survive without your attention for a week."

"What—no laptops? Do they have cell reception up there?"

"No, and no. The only thing you're allowed to pack that has any kind of battery is your vibrator. But we'll be too busy having other kinds of fun to think about sex. Building campfires, roasting marshmallows, running away from bears—"

"Bears?"

"Just kidding. They do have black bears in that neck of the woods, but Lilly says as long as we keep a clean campsite, they'll leave us alone. Are you in?"

I rolled over and pulled my duvet over my shoulders.

"Arghh. I suppose so. As long as I can bring my comforter with me."

"No way," Hannah said. "We have to pack light, just the necessities. We're going to be carrying everything in and out on our back, including the canoes. Three tents, some air mattresses, sleeping bags, and a minimum of provisions. We'll catch everything else we need."

"Fine. As long as I don't have to clean the fish."

Hannah chuckled.

"Lilly's our designated cook. She grew up not far from where we're going. She'll show us how to catch, clean, and cook everything."

Hannah paused for a moment over the line.

"Are you going to be able to drag yourself out of bed at five a.m. this Wednesday to catch the early flight?"

"Go away!" I said, pulling the comforter over my head. "I'll call you later today to finalize the arrangements."

"Atta girl. You're gonna love this. The sky is so clear at night, it practically looks like cream, there are so many stars. It'll be just us girls and the cry of the loon over the still water."

"And bears. Don't forget about the bears."

Early Wednesday morning, Hannah picked me up at my place and we drove to O'Hare airport together. She was excited about the trip, but I was still having second thoughts about going away with so many people I knew. No one yet knew about my recent lesbian experiences—not even Hannah—and I wasn't sure if I'd be able to hide my attraction to six scantily-clad women alone in the wilderness.

"You've been awfully quiet lately," she said, glancing at me watching the cars go by.

"I've just been doing a lot of thinking lately. You know, after the divorce, it's been a little...strange. Not knowing what to do with myself, not having anybody to share intimate moments with..."

"Well nothing's going to happen staying holed up alone in your house, that's for sure. You've got to get back on the horse. I've been trying to take you out to the bar for quite a while now—"

I shook my head and sighed.

"That's just not my scene anymore, Han. I'm getting too...*old* for those pick-up routines."

Hannah took her eyes off the road for a moment and stared at me.

"But you still like *men*, right? I hope you haven't lost your mojo. You're just reaching your sexual prime—"

"It's still there. I guess I'm just looking for the...right one."

"Well let's not worry about any of that for a few days. It's just going to be us girls in the middle of nowhere, with no one around for miles. We don't need no stinking men where we're going!"

I huffed an awkward chuckle, then looked out my window at the passing traffic.

The drive north from Toronto into the Canadian interior was stunning. I marveled at all the pretty rivers and lakes alongside the highway, dotted with pretty boathouses and motor yachts plying the dark blue water. The landscape got increasingly rugged the further we got from the city, and about halfway to our final destination we stopped at an outfitter's to rent two canoes. We chose the top-of-the-line skiffs made of fiberglass and kevlar, and I was surprised how easy it was to lift them up and strap them to the top of our big SUV.

Lilly sat up front while Hannah provided navigation using a crumpled old map from her childhood. Bonnie and Madison, who I already knew from my previous job, sat in the middle seat, while I sat in the rear jumper seat with the new girl, Emma. It was hard keeping my attention focused on the passing scenery with her downy legs poking through skimpy cargo shorts rubbing against me on the cramped bench.

She was a little younger than the rest of us, somewhere in her late twenties I estimated, but absolutely gorgeous. Long corkscrew-curly hair tumbled over her plump youthful cheeks and pretty rosebud lips. She reminded me of the college girl Abby, and I kept stealing glances at her exposed legs whenever she peered out her window.

"Everything okay back there?" Hannah called from the front seat, peering into the rearview mirror. "Jade, are you and Emma getting caught up? You're the only ones who don't really know each other. I hope you guys are making friends—we've got a long trip ahead of us."

"Emma's a doll," I said, stealing another quick glance at her. "We've been pointing out our favorite boathouses along the way. This really is God's country up here."

"You haven't seen anything yet," Lilly said, from the front seat. "What 'til you get to Algonquin Park. It's even *more* beautiful up there. No boats, no cars, and no people. Just the quietest, most serene lake country you'll ever experience."

"How did you know about this place?" Madison chimed in from the middle seat.

"My grandparents had a cottage on Lake Muskoka, not too far from here. I used to spend every summer there growing up, water-skiing during the day, lying on the dock to get a tan, entertaining friends at night. My granddad was the one who taught me how to fish. There's nothing like the taste of fresh-caught smallmouth bass cooked in a skillet with nothing but butter. You guys are going to die and thought you'd gone to heaven."

"If I don't die first watching you cut its head off," I joked.

The last few miles to our embarkation point took us along a narrow gravel road through thick maple and birch trees. We could hear the overhanging branches scraping against the hulls of the overturned canoes on the roof of our car, and I smiled at Emma when she reached over and grasped my hand in excitement. The road terminated in a thicket by a small parking lot, and we locked our car near a beat-up old Pathfinder, then lifted our heavy backpacks loaded with provisions onto our shoulders.

Lilly and Hannah took the lead carrying the first canoe, while Bonnie and Madison followed close behind carrying the second one. Emma and I took up the rear, keeping a nervous watch out for bears. The trail was narrow and rough, with plenty of dips and boulders to navigate. I was glad I'd brought my hiking shoes as I stepped gingerly over the slippery moss-covered rocks.

"Are we there yet?" I called ahead to Hannah and Lilly, only half-kidding.

"It's about thirty more minutes to the main lake where we'll put in," Lilly said. "But there's a pretty waterfall about halfway where we can rest and freshen up."

"Suck it up, trooper," Hannah said. "Don't be a pussy. We haven't even got to the hard part yet. Enjoy the scenery. Can't you smell the fresh scent of the Great White North?"

"I thought that was the scent of your stinky armpits," I joked.

Fifteen minutes later, we began to hear the distant sound of a waterfall as the trail began to get steeper and more treacherous. The girls carrying the canoes had to walk carefully so as not to lose their footing and topple the canoes from their shoulders. I suddenly felt guilty about not carrying my weight.

"Do you guys need a third?" I shouted ahead. "Those canoes look pretty heavy. I'm happy to lend another shoulder."

"It's actually easier to maneuver with two than three," Lilly said. "But after our rest stop, I'll be happy to switch if you're still game. It's getting a bit hot under here. I could use some fresh air."

The sound of falling water grew louder and louder until we came upon a small, sloped waterfall at the side of our trail.

"Let's stop here and cool off for a bit," Lilly said. "Do you guys feel like a refreshing shower?"

"Hell, yes!" Hannah said, as she and Lilly lifted the canoe off their shoulders and lowered it to the ground.

I looked at everybody's cargo pants, fleece vests, and heavy hiking boots.

"Aren't we a little overdressed?" I said.

"It's just us girls out here," Hannah replied, beginning to strip off her outerwear. "Who needs clothes?"

She and Lilly stripped down to their bra and panties, then they paused and looked at the rest of us playfully.

"Fuck it," Hannah said. "There's no one around. Let's go au naturel."

The two girls unclasped their bras then pulled their panties off and scampered into the waterfall, laughing as the water splashed against their bare chest and asses.

"What are you guys waiting for?" Hannah said, looking at the rest of us hesitating on the bank of the waterfall. "It's warm, clean, and refreshing. Strip off your clothes and join us!"

The four of us glanced at one another for a few seconds, then we quickly disrobed and joined Hannah and Lilly in the waterfall. At first it was a bit of a shock feeling the cool water on my hot skin, but it didn't take long to get used to it. After a few minutes, it felt just like a warm shower.

I'd barely had a chance to glimpse at the naked bodies of the other girls before they scrambled into the waterfall, but with the running water tumbling over us, it was a feast to take in. We were all in good shape from regular yoga and gym classes, but there was something about Emma's figure that I couldn't take my eyes off. She had a more slender, youthful figure, and I stole glances at her pointed nipples on her perky breasts as the water cascading over her tight chest and abdomen. Her bare pussy shined in the sunlight as the liquid fingers teased and danced over her glistening mound.

"What'd I tell you?" Hannah said, blinking at me as the water crashed over her head. "Isn't it glorious? Warm, refreshing, and *unspoiled*."

Lilly tipped her head as she opened her mouth wide under the falling water.

"Feel free to rehydrate," she gurgled. "This is the cleanest water you'll find just about anywhere on earth. Lop it up!"

We all tilted our heads back and giggled and spat at one another as we stretched our arms out, feeling the warm current passing over us. After a few minutes, Lilly began tiptoeing over the steep rocks lining the waterfall toward the other side of the cataract.

"Come on, you guys," she said. "There's something else I want to show you. Just be careful as you step on these slippery rocks. I don't want anybody falling down the waterfall."

"Um, *yeah*," I said, glancing down the steep embankment to the bottom of the waterfall thirty feet below.

We followed Lilly through the falling water, grasping onto the sides of exposed outcroppings to make sure we had a firm handhold and stepping carefully onto the rocks to be sure we had a solid footing. When we all got to the other side, she giggled and ran off into the bush. We had no idea where she was going, but after about twenty feet through the thick brush, we stopped at the top of a sheer cliff overlooking a lake thirty feet below.

We stood there for a moment trying not to gape at each other's wet naked bodies, then peered at Lilly warily.

"What do you say?" she said. "Are you guys game?"

"What?!" Madison exclaimed. "You mean *jump*? Off *this*? Down *there*?"

"Are you *crazy*?" Bonnie said. "We'll *kill* ourselves!"

"It's only thirty feet or so," Lilly said. "I've done it plenty of times. It doesn't even hurt. Just be sure to put your hands over your peachka and keep your legs together so you don't get too much of a slap between your legs. Last one in is a pussy!"

Lilly screeched as she jumped off the cliff while we peered over the ledge and watched her splash into the still water below. Five seconds later, she emerged from under the surface and screamed with delight as she motioned for us to follow.

We all looked at one another with wide eyes, then Hannah, Bonnie, and Madison followed soon after. I glanced at Emma with a mix of trepidation and lust. Part of my hesitation was not wanting to be the last one following the girls into the pool below, but the other part of me just wanted to stay on top and take in Emma's sweet nubile body as long as I could. She kept her body shyly turned away from me so I couldn't see her bare mound while she quivered holding her arms tightly across her chest. The other girls were taunting us from below and I knew that sooner or later one of us would have to go.

"Are you up for this?" I said, watching her quaking in fear.

"I dunno," Emma said. "It's a long way down."

"How about if we hold hands and do it together?" I said.

Emma looked at me uncertainly for a moment, then nodded and edged closer to me. Then she held out her hand and I clasped it gently. I could feel her hand shaking, and I squeezed it to build her confidence.

"On the count of three, okay?" I said.

Emma nodded as I began the count.

"One...two...*three!*" I yelled as Emma and I leaped off the cliff together into the bracing water below.

That wasn't the only leap that Emma and I would take over the next few days.

2

NIGHT WHISPERS

We swam for a few minutes in the warm water of the lake below the waterfall, then retrieved our gear and completed our portage down to the shore. The experience of paddling the canoes across the quiet lake was sublime. There was virtually no noise other than the occasional cry of a bird and the soft sloshing sound of our paddles dipping in and out of the water. Little black bugs skittered over the surface as the bows of our canoes sliced through the shimmering liquid. Every now and then I'd hear a droplet sound near our boat followed by little concentric ripples in the water.

"What's that sound?" I asked Lilly, who'd taken up the stern position in my canoe. "It sounds like someone throwing pebbles in the water."

"It's fish feasting on all those water skeeters," she said. "They're a pretty tempting snack just sitting there on the surface."

"What *kind* of fish?" Hannah asked, peering over the gunwale into the dark water from her squatted position in the middle of our canoe. "Should we be worried about us being fish food for some kind of monster dwelling under the surface? It's pretty dark down there. I can barely see two feet below the surface."

Lilly chuckled as she dragged her paddle in the water to steer our canoe gently to the starboard side.

"The water's actually remarkably clear when you're underneath it. But you needn't worry about any Jaws-like predator under the surface. It's mostly filled with Walleye, Pike, Bass, and Yellow Perch. Though some of the Muskies do grow to five or six feet in length, they only have teeth big enough to eat smaller fish."

Hannah peered over to the other canoe knifing through the water a few feet away.

"What about *Emma*?" she said, smiling at the cute girl next to us. "By those standards, I'd say she qualifies as 'smaller fish'. You better watch out you don't get gobbled up by one of those things, Emma!"

Emma turned her head in Hannah's direction and peered over her sunglasses, then continued quietly paddling the front of her canoe. I watched her toned arms rippling and her little breasts shaking on her chest as her ass wiggled on her seat from the paddling motion.

"Where's a good place to set up camp?" I asked Lilly.

She looked around the lake and saw a small rocky outcropping about half a mile to our northeast.

"There's an island over that way," she said pointing to the peninsula. "We should have it all to ourselves, and if I remember correctly, there's a quiet little bay behind it that should make for perfect bass fishing. We can all give it a try later and see if we can catch something fresh for dinner."

"When you say all to *ourselves*, do you mean no bears?" I asked.

Lilly chuckled at my first-time camping trepidation.

"I meant in terms of other campers. We probably won't run into anybody else this far from civilization, but I did notice another car in the parking lot at our trailhead. As for bears, they're pretty good swimmers, but as long as we keep our food locked up and sealed, they should leave us alone."

"I'm not sure I'm comfortable with the *should* part of that statement," I said.

When we got to the island, we found a small beach and pulled our canoes ashore. We unpacked the boats and located a flat mossy section in the center of the island to pitch our three tents. There were six girls, with each tent comfortably accommodating two air mattresses and two sleeping bags. We contemplated drawing straws to see who would sleep with whom, then we all just giggled and threw our gear in whichever tent was closest. Hannah joined me, Maddie and Lilly took the next, and Emma and Bonnie took the last. I peered over at Emma's tent as she got down on her knees and wiggled her ass through the front canopy, suddenly wishing I'd joined her.

After we set up camp, we set out in pairs to collect kindling and driftwood for a fire, then we had a refreshing swim in our bikinis to cool off. I was surprised how hot it got by mid-afternoon, and the water, though still warm, provided a handy respite from the heat. Soon after, Lilly collected the fishing rods and tackle, and we all walked over to the far end of the island overlooking a small bay filled with water lilies.

"Now I see why you like to come here," Hannah chuckled, scanning the idyllic scene. "It's filled with your favorite type of flowers."

"Yeah, well those lilies also provide perfect cover for bass and perch. We've got our own little seafood restaurant hiding under those pretty flowers."

She reached down onto the ground and picked up a fishing rod.

"Who knows how to use these things?"

We all just looked at her dumbfounded.

"No worries," she said. "Let me show you how it's done."

She connected the loose pieces of the shaft then attached a red and white striped metal lure to the end of the fishing line. Then she stepped about ten feet back from our group and looked out over the shore.

"Okay," she said. "The most important thing is that you don't snare yourself or anyone else as you're casting your line into the water. Which is why you'll need to separate yourself from your next nearest fisherwoman by at least ten to fifteen feet."

"Fisherwoman?" I teased. "Is that what your grandpappy used to call you?"

"Not exactly. But hey, there's no guys out here, so I'm improvising. Fisherperson, fisherman, angler, whatever. Now listen up. After I get your rods and lures assembled, you hold the rod like this."

Lilly held the rod out firmly in front of her, gripping the cork handle.

"Like you're giving it a firm handshake, with your middle and forefingers threaded under the handle of the reel."

"Or like you're giving it a firm hand job," Hannah snickered.

"Now..." Lilly continued, rolling her eyes. "Hold the rod out beside you and make sure you've got about two feet of line hanging down from the tip of the rod, like this."

"Like a horny cock dripper..." Hannah said, continuing the metaphor.

"Behave, Hannah," Lilly admonished her friend, "or I'm gonna slap your ass. Now, press and hold this little release button on your reel, then turn your body sideways, holding the rod out in front of you. Then swing your arm quickly out in the direction you want your lure to land and release the button just before you get to the end, like this."

Lilly deftly swung the rod with her wrist and we watched her lure sail about forty feet over the water and plop just short of a bunch of water lilies.

"I'm attaching bobbers to the ends of your lines so you shouldn't have to worry about your line getting caught on rocks underwater."

"*Bobbers*? *Rods*? *Swinging*?" Hannah joked. "You gotta admit it sounds a bit like—"

"Put your dick in your pants, Hannah," Lilly said. "Try to concentrate, will you, so we all don't starve out here?

"When you cast your lure," she continued, "try not to get too close to the flowers or your line will get caught up there too. You may need to practice a few times to get the hang of it, but after a few swings, you should be casting like a champ. After your lure lands in the water, start turning the crank on the reel counterclockwise slowly so your lure will swim through the water looking like a real fish."

"What if we *catch* something?" Bonnie asked.

"You'll feel a tug on your line and some sudden tension in your reel. Just steady your rod and crank the fish in slowly toward shore. Give me a shout if you need any help. Once your fish gets close to shore, I'll use my net to land him. Then I'll tie him up to this little stringer to keep him fresh underwater until we eat."

"Until you chop off his head and gut and cook him, you mean," Hannah joked.

Emma hunched her shoulders and winced.

"Poor little fishes," she said. "They'll just be going about minding their own business when suddenly a hook tears into their flesh. Then we'll yank them by their mouth out of their element and tie them up while they wait to be guillotined. How barbaric!"

"Hey, it's a fish-eat-fish world out there, Emms," Lilly chuckled. "We just happen to be the biggest fish at the top of the food chain. If I remember correctly, we don't have any vegetarians among us, do we?"

Lilly paused for a moment to make sure everybody was on board.

"Right, let's get started then. If anybody wants to sit this one out and just watch the rest of us, that's cool. If we're feeling generous, we might share some of our catch with you later."

Lilly proceeded to assemble each of our rods, then we separated along the bank and awkwardly practiced casting into the bay. It didn't take me too long to get the hang of it, and after five or six casts I was able to fling my lure almost as far as Lilly with similar accuracy. I glanced over at Emma standing fifteen feet to my right and noticed her huffing and cursing as her lure jerked and plopped into the water only a few feet in front of her.

I stepped behind her and reached around, grasping her rod with my two hands.

"Hey, Emma," I said. "Let me see if I can help you. The key is in timing the button release at the right moment."

I positioned Emma's thumb over the button on the reel, then placed my thumb over hers. Then I pulled the rod gently behind us a few feet and swung her arms forward in a sudden jerk.

"*Release!*" I yelled as we watched her lure go sailing twenty feet into the bay.

"Yayyyy!" Emma squealed with delight.

Then she turned around and kissed me on the cheek.

"Thanks, Jade. You're an awesome fisherwoman. Don't go too far away. I still might need you to show me how to wiggle my hips properly to make this work."

I looked into Emma's eyes and smiled as I felt my cheeks warm with a gentle flush.

"You got it, girl," I said. "I'll keep one eye on you from my perch right over there."

Truth was, I kept more than one eye on her wiggling ass in her tight bikini as she continued casting her rod. After about ten minutes of quiet casting into the still waters of the bay, Emma suddenly began hyperventilating.

"I think I've got something!" she squealed, as we watched the tip of her rod twitch and bend in frenetic tugs.

"Okay, Emm," Lilly said, rushing over. "Just hold your rod steady and slowly crank the handle of your reel away from you. There's no rush—let him tucker himself out for a bit before you try to outmuscle him."

She looked at the deep bend in Lilly's rod and nodded.

"It looks like a big one, maybe a five-pounder. That might be enough to feed all of us tonight. Be cool, girl—take your time. Just remember, you're stronger than he is."

We all cheered Emma on as she struggled to control her fluttering rod and awkwardly reel in the fish. When it got close to shore, it jumped two feet out of the water and waved twice rapidly in the air before diving back under the surface.

Lilly stepped down onto the bank with a fishnet and stepped into the water as the fish neared shore, then swung the net underwater and lifted it up for us to see. As the bass flapped wildly in the tangled rope, Lilly calmly reached down and removed the hook from its mouth. Then she threaded her fingers under its gills and held the fish up for everybody to see.

"Woo-hoo!" Emma yelped, proud that she'd caught the first fish of the day.

"Good job, Emm," Hannah said, and we all clapped and smiled to acknowledge her accomplishment.

Lilly attached Emma's catch to the stringer chain underwater, then the group fished for another thirty minutes until we'd caught three more bass.

"That should do it if you guys want to take a breather," Lilly said, placing the stringer of fish in a metal pail filled with water. "Time to cook these fellas up and see what real Canadian food tastes like."

The sun was beginning to lower on the horizon, and after taking another short swim to cool off, we all got dressed in cargo pants and polar fleeces to protect ourselves against the mosquitos and evening chill. I watched Lilly deftly cut off the head of each fish then expertly fillet the flesh to remove it from the thin skeleton underneath.

"Looks like you've done this before," I said, marveling at her skill.

"A few hundred times maybe," she said.

I stood mesmerized as she sliced the fish under its belly and removed its entrails, then carefully pulled the flanks away from the spiny skeleton inside.

"Kind of messy, huh?"

"Yeah, it's a bit gross at first, but you get used to it pretty quick. My mouth is already watering thinking about the taste."

While Lilly filleted the fish, the other girls collected some small logs and rocks from around the shore and placed them in concentric circles in the middle of our campsite to build a fire pit. Then they placed some twigs and driftwood inside the rocky pit and started a small fire. After it quieted down a bit, Lilly placed a steel grate and a cast iron pan over the hole and slapped a few slivers of butter in the pan along with the fillets. Before long, the aroma of fresh pan-seared fish wafted into the air.

"That smells exquisite, Lilly," Hannah said, suddenly emerging from her tent. "Do you need us to help prepare any sides?"

Lilly shook her head.

"For our first night together, I just want you to savor this, straight-up. All we need to finish it off is some lemon slices cut up and some paper plates and forks."

When the fish was done, we all sat around the campfire on the wooden logs while Lilly served us our plates.

"*Oh my God,* Lilly," Bonnie said, placing the first morsel in her mouth, closing her eyes and tilting her head back. "This is to *die* for! Now I don't feel nearly as bad about yanking those little critters out of their cozy lily garden."

"What about *you*, Emma?" Lilly said, glancing in her direction. "Are you comfortable with eating your catch?"

"Um, *yeah*," Emma said, as she gobbled the fish down.

"Mmmm," Hannah chimed in. "What *is* it exactly that makes this so good? This tastes even better than at the top-rated seafood restaurant in the city."

"Who knows?" Emma said, shaking her head. "It could just be because we're eating it truly fresh-caught. Maybe it's the lemon and butter seasoning."

"Or maybe it's just that pristine freshwater Canadian goodness coming through," I joked.

After we finished eating, Lilly placed the entrails and fish heads back in the water, then we washed our cutlery and bagged up our plates and hung our trash from a rope over a high tree branch to keep the bears away. As dusk set in, we built our fire back up and huddled around the pit in a circle.

"What now?" Hannah said. "What do six girls do for fun after dark on a lonely island in the middle of nowhere? Tell spooky stories?"

"*Stories* could be fun," Maddie said. "But they don't have to be spooky. I'm already creeped out enough about the idea of sleeping in that flimsy tent with so many bears within swimming distance. How about some *fun* stories?"

"I know!" Bonnie said. "Let play *Truth or Dare*. That outta get our juices going. Who wants to go first?"

"Truth, or *dare*?" Hannah asked.

"Truth," Bonnie said. "Tell us something daring about yourself that none of us know."

"Hmmm," Hannah said, looking up trying to think of some sordid detail from her past that she was willing to share. "Well—I once spent a night in jail."

"No way!" Emma said, her eyes widening in disbelief.

"*Way*," Hannah said. "Though granted it was only for a couple of hours. I was sixteen and got caught for shoplifting. I think the sheriff in my small town wanted to make an example of me to scare the shit out of me."

"Did it work?" Lilly asked.

"I wasn't really scared, because I was all alone in my cell and I kind of knew what they were trying to do. I was more scared about what my father was going to do to me when he bailed me out."

"And?" I said.

"Grounded for three months. Which is like three *years* when you're sixteen. So yeah, I guess it worked insofar as discouraging me from doing something like that again."

"What did you steal?" Bonnie asked.

"A vibrator from the local sex shop. I was too embarrassed to actually buy it, so I tried to sneak it out under my coat instead."

"That'll teach you to play with naughty things before your time," Lilly winked at Hannah.

"What about *you*, Lil?" Hannah said. "What naughty things have you done that we don't know about?"

"*Welll*," Lilly said, stretching out the word for dramatic effect. "I engaged in some technically illegal sex not too long ago...."

"Mmmm, *yummy*," Hannah said. "Do tell. There's not many things that are illegal anymore in that area."

"It was an underage boy. *Sixteen* to be exact. The captain of my son's football team. We were at the boy's parents' house celebrating their championship and he and I were alone having a chat, and one thing led to another. We slipped into the ravine behind his yard and had a quickie."

"A *quickie*?" Hannah teased. "That hardly sounds like fun. Was he nicely hung at least?"

"He definitely came equipped with a decent package. But you know boys at that age. They can't last very long—"

"What exactly did you two do?" I probed for more details.

"I just gave him a quick blowjob. I was too terrified we'd be found out. But it was fun and definitely satisfying."

"For at least *one* of you!" Madison said.

"I suppose," Lilly said. "How about you, Maddie? What kinky things have you gotten into that we don't know about?"

Maddie paused for a moment trying to conjure up a sufficiently juicy story.

"Well, my husband and I just had anal sex for the first time last week—"

"Which *one*?" Hannah said. "You or *him*?"

"*Hannah*!" Bonnie scolded, shooting Hannah a disapproving look. "That's prying a little too deep. Let Maddie tell the story."

"What?" Hannah said. "I'm just saying, she could have used a strap-on, or something. Some guys are into that sort of thing—"

"It was *me*, if you must know," Maddie said. "I mean *receiving*, that is."

"What's that like?" Emma said, scrunching up her nose in disgust. "I mean, doesn't it hurt?"

"Oooh," Hannah teased. "I guess we know at least *one* of us has never tried this. Poor little Emma, leading such a sheltered life..."

Emma lowered her head and frowned as she peered into the fire. I wanted to walk over to her log and put my arms around her. It was cruel of Hannah to put her on the spot like that and make her feel small.

"Well it didn't hurt exactly," Maddie continued. "But I wouldn't say

I enjoyed it as much as the usual way. My husband certainly did though, judging by his moans of delight."

Everybody paused for a moment as the girls looked at me and Emma to see who would go next. Hannah glanced over at Emma still sulking on her log and finally broke the silence.

"What about you, Jade? What kind of fun adventures have you been up to lately? I mean besides sleeping in and working on your graphic design projects?"

I looked at Hannah with a sly smile. If she *only* knew. I probably had accumulated enough kinky stories just in the last couple of months to outdo everybody around the campfire. But I still wasn't ready to share my most personal secret.

"Well, I recently had a little remote affair with one of my neighbors..." I started.

"*Remote*?" Hannah said. "As in not face-to-face? Was it telephone sex or webcam sex?"

"Neither. We just watched each other through our windows at night. It was actually pretty hot."

"Oh? Is this someone you've had your eye on for a while? Is he hot? What did you guys do?"

"Yes, I've had my eye on him for a while now," I lied, not wanting to tell the girls that it was actually Abby, the college girl next door. "We've been watching each other around our adjoining pools for some time. But he's married, so I never felt comfortable making the first move."

"So, what did he do? Flash you from his private study while his wife was doing the dishes?"

"I think his wife was away for a few days. It was late at night, and I caught him coming out of the shower with his bedroom light on. I guess he caught me watching him and one thing led to another..."

"So you both rubbed one out watching each other?"

"Yeah. But it was just a one-time thing. His wife came home the next day and I didn't want to take any more chances at getting caught."

"Well that definitely qualifies as semi-hot," Lilly said.

Everybody turned to Emma, who glanced nervously out of the corner of her eyes at the rest of the group.

"That just leaves you, Em," Lilly said. "What sordid details have you been holding back about yourself?"

Emma paused for a long moment as she glanced at her friends around the campfire.

"Well, I once did it with a...*girl*. You know, at college."

My panties instantly moistened as I squirmed uncomfortably on my log.

"It was with my roommate. We were both pretty drunk after a party, so I'm not even sure it qualifies—"

"Oh, I think it *definitely* qualifies," Hannah said. "You've got to give us at least a few details. What did you two do exactly?"

"You know, the usual stuff. There's only so many things two girls can do together, right?"

"*Boo!*" Hannah jeered. "Not good enough. You've got to give us at least one detail."

"Well," Emma hesitated. "It started with us both lamenting how neither of us had hooked up in a long time. One thing led to another, and we ended up making out on my bed."

The more I listened to Emma, the more I could feel a large wet spot spreading in my cargo pants between my legs. I shimmied toward a knot on my log and quietly rubbed my clit against the stump in the dark as Emma told her story.

"*Making out?*" Hannah said. "What do you mean? Kissed, fondled, sucked, scissored—we want details!"

I could see Emma shifting nervously on her log, beginning to feel uncomfortable about sharing any more details.

"You know," I interrupted. This whole time we've been telling truths and we haven't even had a single dare. I've got a dare for every-body. I dare you all to strip off your clothes and go skinny dipping in the lake with the big old muskies and snapping turtles!"

"If we don't get eaten alive by the *mosquitoes* first!" Bonnie protested.

"Not if we get in the water fast enough," I said, stripping off my clothes. "Last one in a rotten egg!" I scampered over the pine needles of our campsite and ran into the water at our little beach.

"Come on in, you scaredy-cats!" I taunted from the water. "The water's warmer than the air. It's like taking a bath."

The rest of the girls quickly disrobed and scurried into the water, where we splashed and spit water at each other's faces and playfully dove under the surface groping each other. After about ten minutes, we all scampered out of the water and toweled dry, then rushed into our tents and zipped up the flaps to keep the mosquitoes out.

I scolded Hannah for putting Emma on the spot earlier, then we talked a little bit about work before falling asleep early from all the sun and fresh air. But about thirty minutes later, I woke to the sound of rustling not far from our tent. Thinking it might be a bear foraging through our camp, I was about to wake Hannah when I heard the unmistakable sound of a woman moaning. I lay perfectly still and held my breath straining to listen.

The sound was coming from the direction of Bonnie and Emma's tent. I lifted the privacy flap up over the mosquito net window on my side of the tent and peered into the darkness. They'd left a small flashlight on inside their tent, and I could see the shadows of two figures lying next to one another, rubbing their bodies together.

They're making out! I thought.

Suddenly, I wished I'd tried harder to pair up with Emma in her tent. I was envious of Bonnie having her all to herself. Obviously, Emma's story had gotten more than just *me* worked up, and after they'd returned to their tent stark naked, one thing had led to another.

Fuck! I whispered out loud, thrusting my hand under my sleeping bag, beginning to circle my clit.

As I strained to catch whatever I could pick up from the tent next door, I began to hear gasps and moans radiating into the still night. I couldn't make out if it was Emma's or Bonnie's voice, or both of them. But it didn't matter. I was insanely turned on just listening to them, trying to imagine what the two of them were doing.

I squinted through the mosquito netting trying to discern their movement, but I just saw a jumbled clump of shadows shifting in the soft backlight. Suddenly, one of the figures rolled on top of the other, and I saw the unmistakable shape of a naked ass raising and lowering onto the person beneath.

Oh my God. Now they're humping each other!

I wanted to dash out of my tent and join the girls in their fun and feel Emma's sweet pussy between my own legs. *Oh—how much pleasure I could give her,* I thought. I sped up the movement of my fingers over my clit, trying to control my breathing and movement so as not to wake Hannah.

Suddenly, the figure on top raised up to a kneeling position and the girl on the bottom pulled her legs up into a bent knee position. Then the girl on top squatted over her and lowered herself onto her partner below. When the girl on top began shimmying her hips, I saw her full breasts swaying in the backlight and realized for the first time that Emma was on the bottom.

Emma doesn't have tits that full and round, I thought. *Bonnie's full-on fucking her!*

I could hear the women's breathing becoming louder and more ragged, building toward a climax. I jammed two fingers into my cunt and began thrusting as hard as I dared without waking Hannah from the squeaking of my air mattress shifting on the soft ground below us.

Suddenly, the moans escalated in urgency, as Emma thrashed her head from side to side in the throes of pleasure.

"Yes, Bonnie!" I heard her whisper. "Fuck me harder. I'm going to come!"

My pussy suddenly clamped down on my fingers as my orgasm washed over me, and I bit my lip trying to stifle my moans.

"I'm coming, Bonnie!" Emma whispered. "Come with me! Fuuuck —I'm coming!"

Bonnie sped up the humping motion of her hips against Emma, then she suddenly stopped as I saw her chest and torso jerking spastically in the soft backlight.

"Uhnnn," she grunted, as she came inside Emma's sweet tight pussy. "Fuck, yes," she said. "I'm coming, baby!"

I twitched and spasmed inside my sleeping bag as I came along with the two girls, trying desperately not to awaken Hannah sleeping mere inches beside me. When Bonnie finally collapsed on top of Emma and their light switched off, I rubbed out two more orgasms before falling blissfully asleep with the warm stickiness between my legs.

3

―――――

BEST FRIENDS

I woke to the cry of a loon echoing over the still lake. Hannah was still sleeping, so I put on some warm clothes and quietly unzipped the front of our tent. Lilly and Madison were huddled around the fire pit with some mugs in their hands and I joined them.

"Morning, Jade," Lilly said. "Did you sleep well?"

"Like a baby. It must be all this fresh air and clean living. Hannah and I fell fast asleep shortly after our swim last night."

"No bear nightmares or intrusions?" Lilly chuckled.

"No, thank God," I said, wondering if Lilly and Maddie had heard the noise from Bonnie and Emma's tent. "Though I *did* hear some other rustling around the camp..."

"Oh?" Lilly said. "It might have been raccoons trying to steal our leftovers."

She looked up at the high tree branch where our garbage bag from last night still dangled twenty feet off the ground.

"Looks like they weren't able to solve our little challenge."

She handed me a steaming mug filled with dark fluid.

"Would you like some hot chocolate? Sorry we don't have fresh coffee, but we couldn't exactly fit a coffee maker in our backpacks."

I nodded at Lilly and took the mug between my two hands to warm my fingers.

"We're really roughing it, eh?" I said.

"Good one!" Lilly smiled at me. "You see—you're already starting to sound like a real Canadian."

I peered out across the quiet lake and marveled at the serene beauty of the landscape. The water was smooth as glass, and the sunrise reflected over the surface in a dimpled crimson glow. Tall evergreen trees rose from the rocky shore surrounding the lake, and there was no sign of movement other than a pair of low-flying geese skimming low over the water.

"It's gorgeous out here. You were right, Lilly. It's just as magnificent as you said it would be."

I took a sip of my hot chocolate, then peered up at her.

"So, what's on the agenda today? More skinny dipping and fish-wrangling?"

Lilly chuckled.

"We'll wait 'til the rest of the girls get up. But I was thinking maybe another canoe ride and some more exploring. There's so much natural beauty to explore up here. We can try trolling for fish in the deep water. Maybe we'll catch a pike or a muskie. That'd be enough to feed us for a whole week!"

I heard the sound of a zipper opening as Hannah stepped out of our tent groggily.

"Morning, sleepy-head!" I called out. "Who's the lazy morning person *now*?"

"Ha!" Hannah said, taking a seat beside me on the log. "We're supposed to be chilling up here, remember? I haven't slept this well in a long time."

"So you didn't hear our little visitor last night?" I asked, probing to see if she'd been woken up by Bonnie and Emma's little play date.

"We had a *visitor*?"

"I just heard a bit of rustling around the camp." I glanced up toward our hanging trash bag. "Lilly thinks it might have been a raccoon trying to reach our little waste receptacle."

"Speaking of," Hannah said. "I think I need to do a little disposal of my own. What's the protocol up here?"

Lilly reached behind her log and threw Hannah a roll of toilet paper.

"Do as the bears do," she said. "There's a small spade over by the tree. If you can dig a shallow hole and bury it when you're done, it'll help keep the place clean for other campers."

"Man—" Hannah huffed, "we really *are* roughing it, aren't we?"

Shortly after Hannah trudged off into the brush behind us, Emma and Bonnie emerged from their tent. I was glad that no one other than me had apparently heard them frolicking last night, as they approached our group tentatively. I poured some hot water from the steaming pot on the fire into two empty mugs, then emptied two packets of hot chocolate mix into the water and stirred it with a small stick.

"Hey, you two," I said, handing them each a mug. "Welcome to the party. Did you sleep well?"

Emma took a seat on the log beside me and glanced at Bonnie out the corner of her eye.

"Yes," she said. "It was very...*relaxing*. Those air mattresses are surprisingly comfortable. How about you guys?"

I didn't think it would be proper to mention the suspected 'raccoon' invasion that disrupted the camp last night.

"Slept like a baby," I said.

I glanced at Emma's bare legs in her cargo shorts and noticed a pink glow.

"I think maybe you got a little too much sun yesterday, Emma."

I reached into my fanny pack and pulled out some sunscreen.

"You might want to put a little protection on. Lilly's suggesting we go for another canoe excursion today. You'll be fully exposed out there on the water."

Emma accepted the bottle and began spreading the lotion across the inside and top of her thighs. I tried not to stare, but her skin blushed and blanched as she pressed her fingers into her soft flesh.

"Actually, you might want to wear your cargo pants to cover up,"

Lilly said. "I can tell you from experience how easy it is to get a nasty sunburn spending the whole day out on the water."

Hannah suddenly interrupted us as she traipsed out of the brush.

"That was fun." She held the toilet paper roll up for everybody to see. "Anybody else need to take a go?"

We all shook our heads and Hannah placed the shovel and roll behind the log next to Bonnie as she sat down beside her.

"So what's the plan for today? More sexy stories and skinny dipping? What else can six girls do in the middle of nowhere?"

Emma and Bonnie shifted uncomfortably on their logs, and the group paused for a moment in awkward silence.

"Lilly suggested a little canoe excursion," I said. "We could explore the surrounding countryside a bit more."

Hannah peered around the lake as she listened to the sound of frogs chirping from the lily pond.

"Doesn't look like there's much more to discover out here than pine cones and bullfrogs."

"We can try to track down one of those *bears* if you're looking for a bit more excitement," Lilly said. "Or maybe some rattlesnakes. There's a lot more interesting wildlife out here than you might imagine. Don't be such a party-pooper, Hannah."

"Rattlesnakes?" Emma said, her eyes suddenly widening. "You didn't mention *those* before heading out."

"I didn't want to scare you guys away. I figured that might tip the balance. But don't worry. They'll give you plenty of warning if you get too close. You've got a better chance of getting hit by a car in the city than being bitten by a snake out here."

She reached behind her log and opened a cooler, then held out a couple of eggs and a pack of bacon.

"But first, who's up for a real woodsman's breakfast? Cooked up real authentic-like on the griddle?"

"Hell, yes!" Hannah exclaimed. "I could eat a moose right now."

After a hearty breakfast of scrambled eggs and pan-fried Canadian bacon, we set out in our two canoes to explore the lake. There were lots of bays and gullies in the meandering shoreline, and I marveled at the quiet and serene beauty of the craggy landscape. Some of the girls tried trolling for fish behind our canoes, but no one caught anything and by midday, our stomachs were grumbling again. Lilly suggested we put in on a larger island to forage for firewood since we'd already collected most of the loose driftwood on our own little islet.

We beached our canoes on the new island and decided to pair up to go exploring. The island was quite large with lots of tall pine, spruce, and fir trees providing ample shade from the hot overhead sun. But the trek was slow-going, with many fallen trees and lichen-covered rocks to sidestep. The girls had decided to pair up again based on their previous tent assignments, and I was beginning to despair of ever finding any alone time with Emma.

We spread out in different directions over the large island. After thirty minutes or so of exploring with Hannah, I caught a glimpse of two bodies reflecting in a shaded glade. I stopped and peered in their direction and realized it was Bonnie and Emma. They were topless and making out behind a large tree! Hannah looked back at me wondering what was holding me up, and I told her I had to stop to take care of some business and that I'd catch up with her.

As she moved further ahead, I slowly crept closer to Bonnie and Emma's position. It was hard to stay quiet with all the loose twigs and rocks on the ground, but I managed to get within about thirty feet of them without being detected. When I got close to their alcove, I ducked behind a large stump and saw that Emma had removed all of her clothing and was sitting on a fallen tree with her legs spread apart. Bonnie knelt between her legs bobbing her head up and down.

Fuck! I thought. *She's licking her pussy! Right in the middle of the forest!*

I quickly dropped my pants and began rubbing my cunt furiously. I had to fight hard to control my breathing and movement so as not to be detected as I gritted my teeth trying to contain my pleasure. Emma arched her back and placed her hands beside Bonnie's ears then pulled her head into her snatch. I could hear her grunting and moaning, and it took every ounce of my energy to remain silent.

As I hunched down behind my tree stump trying to keep my head hidden, suddenly a twig broke underfoot and I ducked under the stump to hide from the girls. I could hear them stop for a moment as they looked around to ensure they were alone, then Emma's moaning resumed. When I peered back over the log, my eyes met with Emma's and we froze for a moment realizing we'd seen each other. But she didn't ask Bonnie to stop and instead pulled her head harder into her pussy as she stared at me through glistening eyes. I kept my head down just enough to stay hidden if Bonnie turned around, while I watched Emma get eaten out.

Emma began rocking her hips and as she pulled Bonnie into her, I could tell that she was close. I raised up just enough for Emma to see my face while I squeezed my breast with one hand and jilled myself with the other. Emma must have noticed my movement and known what I was doing, and the sight of seeing each other getting turned on watching the other, ramped up our arousal even more.

Emma stared straight at me as she began panting louder, then she nodded as if signaling that she was ready. That was all I needed and I gushed all over my fallen pants as I watched Emma's head bob and jerk in quiet climax. After a minute or so, Bonnie and Emma began to get dressed and I ducked under my tree stump to collect myself. For now, at least, this private moment of pleasure would remain between Emma and me.

When I caught up with Hannah, she looked at the wet dribbles on the front of my pants and shook her head.

"Girl, you've got to learn how to shit in the woods properly. The trick is to find a rock or tree stump to support yourself. If you're going to squat down, the least you can do is take your pants off first."

"Yeah," I said. "A tree stump sounds like a good idea. Next time."

"I can't take you anywhere, Jade. We're going to have to get you hooked up right soon before you devolve into a blubbering baby."

I just nodded quietly as I followed Hannah along the trail through the forest.

A fter we collected some firewood, we all reconvened at the beach where we'd set in and built another fire pit. Then we sharpened some sticks and cooked some wieners Lilly had packed in the cooler. Neither Emma nor I talked about what we'd seen, but I noticed her looking in my direction frequently with a knowing smile.

After lunch, we set out again in the canoes and found another tall cliff to jump off, then we cavorted in the water and lay in the sun to dry off. Madison caught a big pike trolling behind her canoe, and when we returned to our little island later in the day, Lilly cooked it up in the skillet and we roasted marshmallows telling more fun stories. I kept glancing at Emma, wondering if we were ever going to have a chance to be alone, but around midnight all of us retired to our regular tents.

After we slipped into our respective sleeping bags, Hannah turned to me and smiled.

"Are you enjoying our camping experience so far?" she asked.

"Yes," I said. "This is nice for a change. It's good to get away. You were right, Han. I really needed this. Thanks for inviting me."

Hannah paused for a long moment.

"Did you have fun on the island today?" she said.

"Um, yes. I enjoyed the hike and the hot dog roast—you know, just communing with the girls..."

"I saw you watching Emma and Bonnie."

"What?" I said, feeling a flush roll over my cheeks. "You mean when I held back to take care of some business?"

"That wasn't the only business I saw you taking care of. It's okay, you know. You don't have to hide it from me. We're supposed to be best friends. If you like girls that way, it doesn't change anything between us."

I hesitated, unsure how best to respond, then exhaled deeply, realizing I didn't need to hide my attraction to women any longer.

"It was just...*hot*, you know? Watching them go at it like wild animals in the wilderness. I couldn't stop looking..."

"I know. Neither could I. You weren't the only one enjoying the show."

I turned my head toward Hannah and looked at her surprised.

"You too? Are you—"

"I still prefer men. But you have to admit, Emma is pretty hot. I've had my eye on her for a while too. I heard you last night listening to them."

I gasped and sat up on top of my sleeping bag.

"You were sure *faking* it pretty well! Pretending to be asleep the whole time."

"How could I? With you moving your hand between your legs so rapidly under the covers and your air mattress squeaking away."

"Why didn't you say something?"

"I didn't want to interrupt your fun. Besides, I was getting just as turned on as you. I rubbed a couple of quiet ones out listening to you and the other girls. Besides, we're friends. I didn't know if you'd wanted to..."

I looked into Hannah's eyes, suddenly realizing how sexy she was. I'd always admired her beauty, but had never thought of it beyond that. But now that I saw her sitting with the soft glow of the moonlight from our open tent window reflecting off her bare breasts, she looked like much more than just a close friend to me.

I leaned over to her side of the tent and kissed her softly on her lips. She shifted her hips closer to mine and we began kissing more passionately, intertwining our tongues in each other's mouths. When she pressed her tits against mine, we both began moaning.

"Damn, girl," she said, pulling away from me for a moment. "Can you believe we've waited all these years to do this?"

Then she crawled out of her sleeping bag and began to unzip the side of my bedroll. She flipped the cover over and straddled my naked body. Then she began kissing my neck and working her way down my body. When she got to my breasts, she sucked on my teats gently, swirling her tongue around my nipples as I held her cheeks gently between my two hands. I tried to pull her up to kiss her again, but she pushed me down on my air mattress and continued nibbling her way toward my pussy. When she got to my belly button she paused, blowing kisses into my little hole, then gently kissed her way to the bony edges of my pelvis.

"For somebody who doesn't like girls," I said, panting in anticipation, "you sure know your way around a female body."

"Who said I didn't like girls?" she said, glancing up at me.

"But you said you prefer—"

"Just shut up, will you?" she said, stretching her hand up to my chin and placing it gently over my mouth. "Lie back and enjoy this. I've been wanting to do this for quite a while."

Hannah extended her tongue and traced a line down the ridge of my hipbone toward my steaming pussy. I lifted my hips, inviting her to go lower, but she paused on top of my mound and rubbed her cheeks softly against my pubis.

"You're so soft," she purred. "Somebody's had some work done recently."

Then she lowered her head between my legs and placed her open mouth directly over my hard clit and began sucking it into her mouth. I moaned and gyrated my hips in pleasure as I ran my fingers through her soft, sun-dried hair.

"Hannah," I moaned. "That feels so good. Don't stop."

"Mmmm," Hannah hummed in assent.

I was enjoying Hannah's attention on my clit and could have come from that alone. But after a few minutes, she started caressing the sides of my labia, then she inserted two fingers inside my sopping hole. I groaned in pleasure, suddenly flashing back to the image of Emma getting eaten out by Bonnie on the log in the forest. I placed my hands beside Hannah's head and pulled her in closer to my throbbing snatch. When she began curling her two fingers against the inside of my pussy on my G-spot, I gasped out loud.

"Yes, Hannah!" I moaned. "Right there. Suck me. I'm going to come all over your pretty face. Make me cum, Han!"

Hannah moaned louder into my pussy and stepped up the pace of her licking and finger movements. I could feel my orgasm welling up inside me and I lifted my hips in preparation for the coming climax. When it poured over me, I couldn't stop screaming out in pleasure.

"Fuck, yes, Hannah! I'm coming, baby! I'm cumming in your sweet mouth. Ohhhh, I'm cumming so hard!"

Hannah held me tightly until I stopped twitching, then she lay back on the foot of my air mattress and scooted her hips up until our pussies were touching.

"Mmmm, Jade," she said. "Your pussy is so warm. I want to fuck you and feel your juices running all over me."

She tried rocking her hips awkwardly against me to create more friction, but I could tell she was getting frustrated trying to generate sustained and steady contact. After a couple of minutes of awkward flailing, I sat up on my air mattress and kneeled over her.

"Let me do this, hun," I said, looking into her eyes.

I placed my right thigh under one side of her hips then lifted my other leg over her stomach until we were in a sideways scissor position with me sitting on top. When I started rocking my hips and grinding our clits together, she gasped.

"*God*, yes! Fuck me, Jade! Fuck my aching pussy. I want to feel you cum all over me again."

"Fuck that," I said. "I want to feel you cum on me. It's your turn to lie back and enjoy my attention. Just focus on the pleasure—"

"Oh, oh, uhnnn!" Hannah panted. "Yes, Jade. That feels so good. Fuck me, honey, with your sweet cunt. Make me cum all over your sweet pussy!"

Hannah began flailing against the side of the tent as she screamed and moaned. I was certain that the whole campsite must have heard what was going on, but neither of us cared. We were so lost in the moment and enjoying our rising pleasure, we would have gladly fucked each other in full view of the other girls right now.

As I listened to Hannah's breathing grow more ragged and her moans increasing in volume, I wondered if Emma was playing with herself like I had yesterday listening to her. Hannah was rocking her hips wildly against me now and tearing at the sides of our tent. I knew she was close and I placed my hands around her hips and dug my nails into the sides of her ass as I pulled her harder against me.

"Now, Han!" I prompted her. "*Come* for me, baby. Let me feel you gush all over my gaping pussy!"

That was apparently all Hannah was waiting for, and she curled her body up toward me and held out her hand. I interlaced my fingers between hers and clasped her hand firmly. I could feel Hannah's grip growing progressively tighter until she finally grunted and exhaled loudly.

"Fuck! I'm *coming*, Jade! I'm cumming all over your sweet cunt. Fuck me, baby!"

I wanted to just focus on Hannah's pleasure and give her a full and proper fucking, but when she spoke those words I couldn't hold back any longer. As I came with her, we both sprayed our juices all over each other's pussies and thighs, screaming and moaning in delight. We shook and spasmed together for almost a full minute as we locked our cunts together in a paroxysm of pleasure.

When we finally collapsed beside each other on my air mattress, we heard the distinctive sound of girls' moaning coming from both of the other tents. We giggled and kissed each other listening to the other girls enjoying each other, then we made love for another hour before falling asleep in each other's arms in my sleeping bag.

4

GROUP FUN

The next morning, we all met around the campfire for hot chocolate. At first, we just made small talk about the scenery and how well everybody was sleeping with all the fresh air. Nobody wanted to broach the subject of what had obviously happened last night in each of our tents. As usual, Hannah was the first to break the awkward silence.

"Well, it's obvious that we were doing a lot more than just *sleeping* last night!"

We all looked at each other sheepishly and smiled.

"I think we should mix it up tonight," she said. "I propose that we change the bunking arrangements. You know, to make it more *interesting*. If we're gonna do this, we should at least *share the spoils*, shouldn't we?"

I glared at Hannah in mock indignation.

"*What?!*" I said. "You've grown *bored* with me already?"

Hannah leaned across our log and planted a big wet kiss on my lips.

"No baby," she said. "I could never grow tired of you. It's just that we only have a few more days out here and we're not going to have too many more chances like this. We can't fit *everybody* in one tent—"

"Hannah has a point," Lilly said, smiling at her partner, Madison. "It's obvious that we were all getting turned on listening to the others having fun. My panties haven't been dry since I heard Emma and Bonnie getting it on two nights ago."

"You *heard* us?!" Emma said. "Why didn't you say something?"

"I didn't want to put you on the spot. I wasn't sure if you guys wanted to share the love. But after last night, I think it's safe to say all bets are off."

We all looked at each other tentatively around the campfire.

"So...who goes with who?" I asked, sensing an argument over who got to sleep with Emma next. "Do we draw lots or something?"

"You make it sound like we're choosing who goes into battle!" Hannah joked. "Besides, we don't just have to stick with *one* partner, do we? We can always move around..."

"You mean play musical tents?" Maddie kidded.

"Something like that," Hannah said.

"I don't think there's any rules for this sort of thing," Lilly interjected. "Let's see how the chips fall. What do you say we work up our appetite a little bit with some more hiking and canoeing? Maybe we can find another waterfall to play in. That should get our juices flowing!"

We all looked at each other excitedly around the fire, contemplating what lay ahead for each of us. When my eyes met Emma's, we lingered a little longer, smiling as we fanned our legs together unconsciously.

"Right, then," Lilly said, reaching into the cooler. "Who's up for some more of that Canadian bacon?"

"I definitely could use a little *meat* right now," Hannah said, winking at me.

<hr>

We spent the rest of the day swimming, fishing, and canoeing around the lake. When we found another waterfall, we took off our clothes and frolicked and washed ourselves in the warm fountain. We rubbed our naked bodies together playfully under the falling water, but nobody made any moves to go further. It seemed like everybody was saving themselves for the main event later this evening. But the few moments I had touching Emma's naked body were electrifying, and I knew that I wanted her all to myself if I could find a way to swing it.

When we got back to our camp, Lilly cleaned and cooked the fresh catch we'd caught that day, then we roasted some more marshmallows while we waited for the first one to make the initial move. Emma kept glancing in my direction, and after a half hour or so she motioned with her head toward the brush. I understood her meaning immediately and excused myself on the pretense of having to relieve myself.

"I think I hear the call of the wild," I said, picking up a roll of toilet paper and standing up off my log. "You girls don't go anywhere. We've still got the whole night ahead of us."

I headed into the bush to do my business, and a minute later Emma stood up and excused herself too. She headed in a different direction into the bush but quickly backtracked in my direction. We met on the fishing bank near the lily pond and giggled.

"Whew!" Emma said, smiling at me. "*That* was awkward. I thought we'd never find a chance to get away!"

"You've felt the same way?" I said, wondering if she felt as strongly toward me as I did toward her.

"Of course! I've been dying to get into your pants ever since the first day when we rode together in the back seat of the rental—."

I leaned in and kissed Emma hard on her lips. We pressed our bodies together and quickly fumbled to take our clothes off. We side-stepped awkwardly towards a tree and I pressed her against the trunk, then reached down and inserted two fingers into her sopping pussy. It wasn't very romantic, but I wanted to fuck her so bad. I pulled my palm up hard against her mound and began finger-fucking her roughly with my hand while I kissed her passionately.

As Emma panted I could hear the sound of her bare back rubbing against the bark of the tree. After a couple of minutes, she pulled away and looked at me.

"Do you mind if we head back to the camp and go into my tent? It's not very comfortable out here, and I'm getting eaten alive by the mosquitoes. Let's go somewhere cozier where we can take our time and do this right. I want to make love to you slowly and feel every part of you."

I looked into Emma's eyes and smiled. She didn't need to ask me twice. I'd been so wrapped up in my own lust, I hadn't noticed that I'd also been stung three times on my ass. We quickly pulled on our clothes and scampered back to the camp. When we got to the fire pit, all of the girls were gone. We looked around and noticed movement in two of the tents. Emma's was the only one that was still, so we unzipped the front and wiggled inside. We tore off each other's clothes then snuggled together into her sleeping bag to warm up from the evening chill.

At first, we just ran our hands over each other's bodies and held each other close trying to warm up in the soft bedroll, while we giggled like two little girls. But it didn't take long for things to heat up. I kissed Emma on her mouth and pressed my tongue between her lips while I ground my hips against hers. When I slipped my thigh between her legs and pressed my knee against her warm box, Emma moaned softly in my mouth. I was surprised how wet she was already. The inside of her thighs were coated with her slick lubrication all the way down to her knees.

I lifted myself up and looked at Emma's pretty face as she sighed from the feeling of my thigh sliding between her legs, then I lowered my face to her chest. I'd been dying to suck on her little breasts from the moment I saw her, and her nipples puckered inside my mouth as she pushed her body against me. I squeezed her tits with two hands as I moved from one breast to the other, savoring the taste of her sweet, tender nubs.

Emma reached down and cupped my breasts while I sucked on her, pinching and rolling my thick nipples between her fingers. I lifted myself up and rolled my tits across hers, feeling our erect nipples rubbing against one another. I could feel her hips rising and swaying in obvious need of attention, and I moved my head further down.

I nibbled on her soft pubis for a few moments, then I kissed my way across her abdomen onto the side of her ass, biting her playfully on her cheek. She turned her body to give me more access, and I gently flipped her over onto her stomach. I could see her magnificent ass in the moonlight, and I cupped and squeezed her buttock muscles, marveling at how perfectly round and tight they were. Then I spread her cheeks and thrust my mouth inside her crack.

Emma gasped when I found her rosebud and began licking around her opening. I knew she was clean because I'd watched her wash herself in the waterfall and noticed that she hadn't gone into the woods since then. She tilted her ass upward and moaned loudly while I squeezed her ass and licked her anus. Then I spread her legs apart and thrust my hand between her legs.

The soft fabric of the sleeping bag was already soaked through from her wetness, and I easily slid my fingers into her slippery hole. As I flicked my tongue over her tender rosebud, I began to thrust my fingers in and out of her pussy. She grunted with each thrust and began wailing in pleasure as I pounded my hand into her.

"Oh! Oh! Oh! she growled, as her body slid forward and back over the air mattress. "Fuck me, Jade!" she said. "Suck my ass!"

I turned my hand over until my palm was facing down, then I slipped the rest of my fingers into her and began fucking her harder. I could feel Emma's pussy opening up inside and knew that she was close to coming. I curled my fingers and trilled her G-spot.

"Fuck, Jade!' she screamed. "Don't stop! Make me cum! I'm going to cum!"

Emma grunted like a wild animal as she pushed her hips down hard onto my hand and squeezed her thighs and buttocks muscles together, burying my face in her ass. I could feel her pussy and anus spasming in hard contractions as she grunted with each pulse. I held her for a few moments, then gently kissed her cheeks as she flopped down onto the air mattress.

A few minutes later, the zipper on the front of our tent opened and Hannah and Maddie stuck their heads through the flap.

"Do you guys want some company?" she said, smiling like a Cheshire Cat. "It sounds like *somebody's* having all the fun in here."

Emma and I looked at one another and laughed.

"The more the merrier!" I said, motioning for them to come in. The girls scampered into our tent but just as Hannah began closing the zipper, Lilly stuck her head in.

"Feel like two more?" she asked.

We all giggled as everybody piled into our tent, and soon after we formed a giant swirling mass of bodies, sucking, licking, and tribbing each other into the wee hours of the night.

***

We fell asleep on top of one another around four a.m. It wasn't until almost midday the next morning when we slowly crawled out of the tent. While Lilly prepared brunch, the rest of us went our separate ways into the bush to relieve ourselves. A few minutes later, Hannah called out from the north side of the island. We all rushed to her thinking she'd fallen or hurt herself, then we saw her crouched down, pointing over the lake.

"Look," she said. "Do you see that?"

I squinted into the distance and saw a canoe with two occupants slowly paddling across the lake, on a parallel course with our island.

"I guess we're not the only ones out here, after all," I said, nodding.

"Can you make out who it is?" Bonnie said. "I mean, are they boys or girls—or one of each? Should we invite them over to share brunch?"

We all looked at each other, hesitating. None of us was sure we were ready to share ourselves with anyone else after last night's orgy.

Hannah suddenly looked in my direction.

"Jade," she said. "Did you bring your binoculars from home? Let's see what they look like close-up. If it's a couple, they might just want to be left alone."

I nodded and hurried back to my tent to retrieve my field glasses from my backpack. When I returned to the group, Hannah took the glasses from my hand as we all crouched down on the mossy ground, spying on the interlopers.

Hannah held the glasses up to her eyes and swiveled the focus button on top.

"Holy shit!" she said. "It's two *guys*. Two very *young* guys!"

"*How* young exactly?" Lilly said.

Hannah paused as she steadied the binoculars over her forehead and adjusted the focus.

"Late teens, early twenties at most. And they're cute! Long hair, a little rough around the edges maybe, but buff!"

"I guess we know at least *one* of us is on board with that," I said.

We all peered over at Lilly and she chuckled as she smiled at us slyly.

"Sounds like the kind of guys who would drive a beat-up Pathfinder," she said, remembering the other car in the parking lot of our trailhead.

Hannah turned around and looked at each of us carefully.

"What do you say, girls? Should we invite them over? I mean, I don't want to spoil our fun, but this could mix things up quite nicely. Think of all the *permutations* this could make. I bet those horny teenagers would jump at a chance to join six sexy girls alone on a deserted island."

We all looked at one another for a moment, then we giggled and stood up on the bank of our island.

"Over here!" Hannah yelled, waving her arms over her head trying to get the attention of the two paddlers. "Come to Momma, you sexy little hunks."

We all jumped up and down on the shore screaming and yelling, and the canoeists stopped paddling for a moment, looking in our direction. Then they looked at one another, unsure of our intention.

"Oh, for crying out loud," Hannah said, peeling off her shirt and bra. "I think they need a little more encouragement."

We all peeled off our tops and jumped up and down on the shoreline, our tits bouncing up and down.

"Here we are!" Lilly shouted. "Six sexy, horny girls! Come dip your paddles in some even hotter water!"

The canoeists suddenly began paddling again, and I saw the boat begin to turn in our direction.

Oh boy, I thought. *Now we've really gotten ourselves into a row of trouble...*

VOLUME THREE

THE HABIT

1

STACKED

I never particularly enjoyed going to the library. Beyond the hassle of dealing with crosstown traffic to get there, it always seemed such a chore to find what I was looking for. Whether I was searching through the card catalogue, the microfilm reels, or even asking the librarian, everything moved at a snail's pace. Having to search through the stacks, access the hard copy, then flip through all the pages to pinpoint my reference material—it all seemed so archaic.

Searching online was so much more efficient. From the comfort of my home office, I could tap in a few search words and within a couple of clicks, get exactly what I wanted. Unfortunately, today, I had no choice but to do it the old-school way. I needed to reference some old newspaper ads to get some ideas for a design project I was working on, and only the library went as far back as I needed.

At least I could count on a relatively quiet environment to do my research. Normally, there were few distractions to get in the way of completing the task at hand. People seemed to respect the rules of public decorum in a library more than other public places like the movie theater or a restaurant. Freed from trilling cell phones and loud side chatter, everybody went about their personal business quietly and politely.

But, today, as I walked toward the microfiche department, something unusual caught my attention. A nun in full regalia stood at the reference desk talking with the librarian. There was something about her manner of dress that seemed out of place among the casual jeans and shorts that other library patrons wore. Her black and white hooded frock stood in sharp contrast to the colorful and largely bare-skinned wardrobe of the other customers.

Like many other bystanders, I caught myself slowing down to stare at her. I saw a few people whispering and snickering amongst themselves as they pointed at her, and I began to feel sorry for the woman. Why should we judge her any differently, I thought, for quietly practicing her faith? There was something admirable about anyone in today's age who could so thoroughly dispense with the material and ego trappings of the modern world.

I was about to continue on my way minding my own business, when the nun turned around. She was much younger than I expected, perhaps in her early twenties, and absolutely stunning. The only part of her that I could see was the front of her face from her chin to her eyebrows. The rest of her head was covered in a white balaclava and hood that draped past her shoulders. She wasn't wearing any makeup, which only seemed to magnify her beauty.

Her pretty face was highlighted with plump rosebud lips, high cheekbones, and soft brown eyebrows. But the feature that stood out most prominently was her eyes. Her irises had an arresting—almost haunting—azure blue color, glimmering like glacial pools surrounded by the snow white hood encircling her head. She could have been a supermodel, and for all I knew, maybe she was. How someone that stunning could turn her back on all the temptations and opportunity that would have fallen into her lap, was a mystery to me.

Now I was even more intrigued by this stranger, and as much as I wanted to respect her privacy, I simply couldn't take my eyes off her. The librarian handed her a piece of paper and as the nun headed in the direction of the stacks, I followed a safe distance behind. Her billowing robe covered her body almost to the floor, but I could tell from the tight cinch of her belt around her waist that she had a slender figure under her heavy clothes.

As she walked toward the stacks, I tried to discern the shape and contour of her body, but her heavy vestments wouldn't betray what secrets lay beneath. But this only added to her allure. It was what I *couldn't* see that made her even sexier. I began to undress her with my eyes, imagining a model-perfect figure to match her face, and bit my lip trying to stifle my rising passion. As my panties began to moisten, I felt ashamed responding to this innocent creature in this way, but I couldn't stop.

Get a hold of yourself, girl, I admonished myself, under my breath.

When she retreated into the narrow space between two tall stacks, I stopped by a chair and placed my hand on the backrest for support. I could hear my breath escalating in excitement and had become weak in the knees. I'd never encountered another person—man or woman—who'd had such a powerful and visceral effect on me. I pulled out the chair and sat down, pretending to look through my purse so as not to be obvious that I'd been following her.

There were some loose textbooks in the middle of the table, and I grabbed one and opened it, pretending to read. I had no idea what the subject matter was because my focus was blurred trying to watch the nun's movement out of the corner of my eye. My pussy was burning in excitement, and I crossed my legs and rubbed my thighs together, trying to give my aching clit some direct stimulation. If there hadn't been so many people around, I would have torn off my clothes and cum within seconds fingering myself.

The nun stood in front of the stack tracing her finger over the spine of some books, trying to cross-reference the call numbers with the paper the librarian had given her. Her eyebrows pinched together in confusion, and for a moment I considered going over to offer some help. But I wasn't sure I could even talk, let alone make any sense, I was so smitten by her beauty. When she leaned forward to take a closer look at one of the books, I squinted to see if I could catch the protrusion of her bosom. But there was nothing to be revealed. It was almost as if she had multiple layers under her clothes to camouflage any hint of her female form.

Those Catholics sure know how to design a uniform to conceal a woman's shape. But I suppose that's the whole point. To minimize the possibility of any temptation—from within or without.

She was wearing a virtually impenetrable barrier to the outside world. My mind began to wander, wondering what kind of undergarments she might be wearing. Was she wearing a traditional corset or a push-up bra? Granny panties or boy-shorts? Nylons or bare legs? Or maybe nothing at all?

You could get away with just about anything under all that get-up, I thought.

I could feel the wetness beginning to spread in the crotch of my tight jeans, and I squeezed my legs together to pull the inseam harder against my throbbing clit. When the nun kneeled down close to the floor to pull a book from the bottom shelf, I couldn't stop myself.

I wish she were kneeling over my face. Oh, how I could give her a taste of earthly delights.

I began to wonder if she'd ever felt the loving touch of another man or woman. Or if she'd even touched *herself*, for that matter. I didn't know much about a nun's vows, but I knew they had something to do with remaining chaste and renouncing most worldly pleasures. It was hard to imagine having no sexual feelings, but if they kept their bodies covered in this manner, it would certainly minimize temptation. The nun never seemed to look beyond her direct field of interest or make eye contact with anyone other than the person with whom she was transacting. Perhaps she'd been trained this way, because there were plenty of scantily clad attractive young men and women scattered about the room to distract one's attention.

Suddenly, she stood up and placed a book under her arm. Then she walked to the rear section of the stacks and turned to walk down the rear aisle beyond my line of sight. After a few moments, I stood up from my desk and went into an adjacent column of stacks to see if I could trace her movement. I pretended to search for a book but instead looked through the space between the shelves to peer through the stacks. I saw her black robe moving to the far rear corner of the library, where she sat down on a large upholstered reading chair.

I grabbed the largest book I could find then headed in the direction of the nun. Not wanting to appear too obvious, I stopped at another upholstered chair about thirty feet away, turned slightly in her direction. I sat down and crossed my legs, then opened the large book on top of my knee. I laughed at my lame attempt at subterfuge, but at least it afforded a modicum of privacy while enabling me to continue spying on my new obsession.

As I peered over the spine of my book at the nun, I struggled to see what she was reading. I couldn't make out the title beyond the large cross appearing on the front cover.

Jesus—is she reading a version of the Bible? Now I'm definitely going to hell for having lascivious thoughts about a devoted woman while she's praying!

But there was no turning back. I was fascinated by this angelic beauty and couldn't take my eyes off her. As she read her book, I studied her face closely from the side. She had flawless alabaster skin, soft rosy cheeks, and a slender, perfectly-straight nose. Whenever she blinked, I could see her long, full eyelashes fluttering over her iridescent eyes. Her expression rarely changed, but every now and then I'd see the edges of her lips curl upwards in a gentle smile as if taken by a passage of her book.

How I'd love to feel those lips smiling around my love button, I thought, feeling my clit tingling in my tight jeans.

The more I looked at her, the more aroused I became, until it was impossible not to touch myself. Having the advantage of elevated padded armrests flanking me on both sides and a large reference book propped up on my legs, I was concealed in my own little cocoon. As long as I was quiet and careful, I could do just about anything I wanted on my chair and no one would be the wiser.

I looked around the room to ensure no one was watching, then I slowly uncrossed my legs and unzipped the front of my jeans and slid my fingers under my panties. But even with the front unzipped all the way, it was hard to reach far enough down into my tight jeans to reach my clit. My fingers pressed against the tight canvas, making it impossible to provide enough room to move around comfortably.

I braced my left arm on the armrest and lifted my hips up slightly, then shimmied my hips just enough to pull my jeans about one inch away from my opening. Now I finally had a little room to operate. My panties were thoroughly soaked, and as I began to circle my clit with the middle finger of my right hand, I had to clench my jaw to stifle my moans. When I redirected my attention back toward the nun, I caught her looking up at me before quickly peering back down at her book.

Shit! I thought. *Had she caught on to what I was doing? She probably runs into all manner of perverts exposing themselves to her whenever she leaves the safety of her convent.*

I froze with my hand down my pants, wondering what to do. The nun seemed to have refocused her attention on her book. My shifting position had probably distracted her temporarily. She couldn't possibly know what I was doing, walled off the way I was. I looked around the rest of the room to make sure I was clear, then slowly resumed fingering my sopping wet pussy.

As I touched myself, I watched the subtle changes in the nun's expression while she read. Her serious countenance made her appear even more model-like, as if she was posing for a camera.

Did she know I was watching her? Did she sense I was turned on by her? If she had, wouldn't she have excused herself?

Was she enjoying being watched?

As I watched her quietly reading, my mind raced thinking of all the dirty things I wanted to do to her if I could get her out of that habit.

What a funny term for a piece of clothing, I thought. I suppose it signifies her taking on a new form of habitual life. Whatever the garment's etymology, I was rapidly gaining a habit of my own for this sexy girl.

Forgive me, Lord. Forgive me the sins of my flesh.

As I began to feel the pleasure rising within me, my legs began to tremble, and I steadied my book on my thighs to disguise what was happening behind my armrests. As I neared my climax, my mouth unconsciously opened and just as I felt my orgasm take hold of me, the pretty nun looked up at me again. She must have known what I was doing from the tortured look of ecstasy on my face, and I looked away in embarrassment.

But I'd passed the point of no return and could no longer hold back the floodgates. As I jilled my clit furiously under my book, I felt the first wave of pleasure sweep over me. I fought to stifle my moans, gagging on the open air with my mouth wide open. I tried to remain as still as possible as the orgasm washed over me, but with each contraction, my chest heaved spastically in my chair.

The fact that I had to disguise the incredible pleasure radiating throughout my body only magnified its intensity. As I sat shaking uncontrollably in my chair, I thought the contractions would never end. I couldn't look at the nun for fear of betraying what was happening, so I peered straight ahead into the blurred text of my book.

When my contractions finally stopped, I slumped down in my chair and exhaled heavily. In my effort to disguise my orgasm, I hadn't realized that I'd been holding my breath the entire time. I panned the room to make sure no one else had witnessed my silent pleasure, then slowly zipped up the front of my jeans.

As I readied myself to silently slip out of the library, I noticed the nun shifting position in her chair for the first time. She crossed her legs and I saw a sliver of skin appearing under her frock above her shoes.

Was she giving me some kind of signal that she knew what I'd done and that she approved? Surely, she'd be discouraged from revealing any more skin in public beyond the small amount of her face?

After a few moments, I noticed a gentle bobbing of her upper foot over her leg.

Was she just indicating that she was happily engaged in her book? Or was this her way of revealing that she was really happy under her habit?

As I peered over the top of my book and watched her more

closely, I noticed that her hips were also squirming in her big armchair.

She's rubbing her thighs together as I was earlier, trying to stimulate her clit!

It was hard to be certain, because she continued staring expressionless straight ahead toward her book, but I noticed her eyelashes were fluttering more rapidly than normal. When her lips suddenly parted a few millimeters, there was no longer any doubt.

She was masturbating herself under her gown in plain view of the entire library! I looked around the room to see if anyone else was paying attention, then looked back at her face. Although she never directly returned my eye contact, the subtle changes of her facial expression and body movements told me everything I needed to know. As she rubbed her thighs together more firmly, her legs began moving more rapidly under her heavy tunic. The bobbing of her foot on her knee steadily picked up pace, and her face began twitching almost imperceptibly.

Suddenly, a deep flush fell over her cheeks and her back pulled away from her chair as the cloth of her habit rippled in shockwaves. She was cumming under her habit, and I was the only one to witness it! I jammed my hand into my panties and came hard again as I plunged my fingers into my soaking snatch. I'd never witnessed anything so sexy in my entire life. As I watched her sitting erect in her chair, spasming from her orgasm, my own pussy clamped down over my fingers in sympathy with her.

Although the pretty nun and I never spoke or made further eye contact that day, something told me this wouldn't be the last I was to see of her.

2

OBSESSION

For the rest of that day, I couldn't shake the pretty nun from my thoughts. It wasn't just her celestial beauty—there was something about her veiled appearance that got me worked up. Now that I knew she had sexual feelings, my mind raced with a million questions.

Was this the first time she'd acted on her impulses? Did she masturbate frequently in the privacy of her own room? Or had she simply gotten turned on watching me play with myself? Did she come to the library often for this express purpose? Was this her only safe outlet for expressing her sexuality? If so, why did she choose to live such a sheltered life, if she harbored such strong earthly desires?

But mostly, I just obsessed about what she *looked* like under all her formal vestments. As soon as I got home, I tore off my clothes and imagined our bodies bending together in every possible position. I imagined sucking her and licking her and fucking her, making her come in every possible way I could conjure. I fantasized about making her moan and scream in ecstasy, as I worshipped every square inch of her gorgeous body.

After I came for about the tenth time that day, I lay in my bed exhausted and naked, thinking about how I might see her again.

Searching for her at the local abbey was out of the question. They probably wouldn't even allow me to *talk* with her, and if so, it would only be through the front gate for a limited time. And my chances of running into her elsewhere in the Chicago area were practically nil. For all I knew, the library may have been the only sanctioned area outside the convent that she was allowed to visit.

My only chance for seeing her again was at the library. I knew that today's encounter might just have been a lucky happenstance, but I hoped that our silent tryst had awoken a primal urge within her that she'd want to revisit. My only hope was that she'd return to the library again soon and that this time we'd have a chance to connect on a more personal level. If so, I had no intention of letting her slip through my fingers again. At the very least, I hoped we could have a coffee together to give me a chance to get to know her a little better. I fell asleep that night imagining her lying beside me, our bodies intertwined, her skin still dewy from making love to me all day long.

The following morning, I headed out early to be at the library for opening time. I didn't want to take any chance that I might miss my blue-eyed nun if she had the same idea as me. If I had to stay there all day every day for a month, I was ready to do whatever it took. I packed my laptop to work on client projects in case she didn't show up, but if she did, I planned to be ready. I wore a mid-thigh skirt and my favorite cream-colored silk blouse, with absolutely nothing on underneath. As I walked up the front steps of the library, feeling the cool morning breeze wafting up against my bare pussy, my nipples hardened, producing two protrusions in my blouse.

If she wants more of this, I thought, *I'll really give her a show today.*

When the library opened, I searched every floor and every corner of the facility, but the nun was nowhere to be found. I hadn't expected to see her right away, so I found an open table near the chair where she'd sat yesterday and flipped open my computer. But as much as I tried to concentrate on my work, I kept glancing over at the vacant chair, thinking about what had happened yesterday.

I glanced around the room to make sure no one could see my computer screen, then I typed in the search phrase *videos of nuns having sex*. I paused before hitting the Enter key, then added the word *lesbian*. I didn't want any men polluting my fantasy. A video titled *Confessions of a Sinful Nun* popped up. I clicked the pause button, then inserted my headphones into the audio jack so I'd be able to listen to the video privately. The video was different from most other pornos, with top-quality cinematography, multiple attractive characters, and a real forty-minute story arc.

This should distract me for a while, I thought.

The video began with the mother superior at a convent informing a young nun that two other nuns had missed communion, asking her to search the surrounding grounds for them. The pretty nun headed out along a trail in the woods, and after a few minutes heard the sound of two women giggling in a sheltered glade. She peered through the branches and saw the two nuns fondling each other under their habits. It didn't take long for them to remove most of their clothing, until they were wearing nothing but white stockings.

As one of the nuns lay on the ground, the other one straddled her face, grinding her bush into the nun's mouth. While she humped the girls face, she turned her body and began fingering the other nun's pussy. Before long, the nun on top began to shake, as her breasts quivered on her chest. "Oh yes!" she said, pulling the other girl's head tighter against her pussy. "Right there!" Just as she came on the other girl's face, the mother superior suddenly walked up behind the pretty nun and asked her if she'd seen anything. The other girls overheard the conversation and quickly scampered away, while the third nun covered for them.

If convent life is anything like this, I thought, *no wonder my blue-eyed nun felt the need to travel so far afield to escape the overprotective clutches of her abbey.*

The video was part of an extended series, and as I watched each clip, I fingered myself quietly under my desk. For over an hour, I took myself to the edge of climax, slowly backing down each time. I wanted to save myself for my *own* special nun if she came back. But when one of the scenes introduced a sister resembling the one I saw yesterday, I couldn't hold back any longer. I was just about to cum when a familiar black and white figure emerged from the stacks about twenty feet away.

It was the same blue-eyed nun from yesterday!

She walked directly past my desk looking straight ahead, carrying another book under her arm. She sat in the same chair as yesterday and opened the book on her lap, then peered up over the binding in my direction. Her eyes widened when she recognized me, then she quickly crossed her legs and directed her attention back to her book. I glanced at the chair I sat in yesterday and was disappointed to see that it was now occupied. But from my vantage point just a little further away, I actually had a more direct view of the nun. And from her seated position directly in front of me, she had a clear view of knees and skirt at crotch level.

This could actually work out better than I expected, I thought.

But as the nun kept her head buried in her book, feigning disinterest, I began to wonder if we'd crossed signals.

Had I frightened her away yesterday with my bold overture? If so, why hadn't she just gotten up and moved to a location where I wouldn't be such a distraction?

When her foot started bobbing again on her knee, her intention became clearer.

What a sly fox. She's signaling her interest in me through her body language.

I closed my computer lid to give her an unobstructed view of my upper body, then unbuttoned two buttons on my blouse to reveal my cleavage. As my breasts pressed firmly against the silk fabric, I could feel my nipples hardening once again. The nun looked up from her book and did a doubletake, before directing her attention back down toward her book.

"Yes," I whispered under my breath. "Did you like that? Give me a little more of your attention, and I'll *really* give you a show."

The nun had her head down, but I could see her long eyelashes fluttering in excitement against her brow. I knew she must have been torn between her vow of celibacy and her desire to engage me more directly.

She just needs a little more incentive, I thought.

I shifted position in my chair and spread my legs two feet apart. A few seconds later, she peered up, and I wobbled my knees under the table to redirect her focus. When her eyes dipped under my desk, they widened in shock when she saw my bare pussy exposed under my skirt. This time, she didn't look away.

As I spread my knees further apart, she stared straight into the junction of my thighs. I reached under the table with my right hand and hiked my skirt up a few more inches. She now had a clear, unobstructed view of my bare, glistening pussy. She froze for a moment, staring between my legs, then peered down again into her book, as a flush fell over her cheeks.

I smiled, knowing how conflicted she must have been between her pact with God and the tug of raging hormones racing through her system. There was something about the frustration she was experiencing that made this even more of a turn on. I looked around the room to make sure no one else was looking, then I placed my fingers over my clit and began to circle it slowly.

If she looks up again, I'll make it impossible for her to turn away this time.

I squeaked my chair, and within a few seconds, the nun's eyelashes lifted above her book again. When she saw my hand between my legs, her leg straightened over her knee and her book wobbled on her lap. As I placed my hand over my vulva and began to rub it over my slit, I could feel my juices spilling out of my pussy, coating my thighs and ass. The feeling emanating from between my legs was sublime, magnified all the more knowing my pretty nun was getting just as wet as me under her heavy habit.

As I began to feel my passion rising, my mouth opened unconsciously, and seeing the look of unadorned pleasure on my face, the nun's lips parted also. Recognizing that we'd made sustained eye contact for the first time, I felt an electric charge go through me, and I pressed my fingers tighter against my snatch. I could have come at any moment, but I wanted to savor this for as long as I could.

When her eyes dipped back under my table, I slipped my middle fingers into my opening and began to fuck myself as my two outer fingers slid up and down the inside of my thighs. I wanted to bring my other hand under the table to massage my clit directly, but it was too dangerous. It would have been far too suspicious for any onlookers to see a woman squirming in her library chair with two hands pumping under the table.

Instead, I pressed the palm of my hand against my mound and shimmied my hand up and down over my button while I pressed my two fingers as deep as I could into my hole. The nun was now bouncing her eyes up and down between my face, my bouncing tits, and my cavitating legs under the table. Her foot began bobbing more rapidly on her knee and I could see the front of her frock rising and falling as she breathed heavily.

For the first time, I could make out the bulge of her breasts under her gown, and although they were heavily concealed by all the layers of fabric, I could tell she had a plump set of tits. As I fantasized about sucking on them, I increased the pace of my finger-fucking and spread my legs wider, until they were almost a full one hundred and eighty degrees apart.

As my orgasm began rising within me, my mouth gaped open and I nodded, indicating that I was about to cum, and the nun did the same. Whether she was feeling the same sensations under her robe, or was simply mirroring my expression in sympathy with me, I wasn't sure. When my climax finally poured over me, I thrust my hand hard against my mound and clamped down over my fingers.

As the pretty nun watched the look of ecstasy wash over my face, I pressed back against my chair and sat shaking in a spastic seizure for a full thirty seconds. When my contractions finally abated, I sat up in my chair with my fingers still embedded in my pussy, savoring the heightened sensitivity inside my warm cavern.

When I finally regained my senses, I realized that I'd been so lost in my own pleasure that I'd temporarily lost focus on what the nun was doing. I wasn't sure if she'd managed to rub one out herself, or if she had just been concentrating on enjoying my show. But when she uncrossed her legs and spread her knees apart, her plan soon became apparent. A few moments later, her right hand disappeared from the edge of her book and I noticed some movement under her gown in the area between her legs as the textbook in her lap begin to shake.

Clever girl! It looked like she'd cut a hole in the side of her frock so she could have direct access to her private areas.

The movement under her gown began to take on a familiar and steady pattern as she began to squirm in her seat. Our eyes met once again, and her lips parted as her chest began to rise and fall more rapidly.

Fuck! I thought. *She's actually going to let me watch her come this time!*

I pushed my fingers harder into my pussy and began shimmying my palm against my clit again. But this time, I paced myself so I could cum with her. As her movements under her robe increased in intensity, I sped up my movements in kind. We were staring directly into each other's eyes now, and I could tell she was getting close.

When she nodded her head to me signaling that she was about to cum, I couldn't stop myself from moaning as my second climax took hold of me. The nun's thighs pulled together as she hunched forward in obvious climax, and I gushed all over my hand as the contractions inside my pussy sprayed my love juices all over my thighs and ass. I clenched my face trying to stifle my moans, but a few pitiful whimpers escaped. At this point, I didn't even care if anybody noticed what I was doing. I was on my own special wavelength with the pretty nun across the aisle, and for now at least, we were the only two people in the room.

After a few seconds, the nun's body relaxed and she lay back against her chair. The book resting on her lap popped up as she pulled her hand from between her legs, then she smiled at me softly and closed her eyes, laying her head on the backrest. I looked around the room to make sure no one else had witnessed our silent affair, then I pulled my sopping fingers out of my cunny and cleaned them with some wet wipes in my purse.

There was no way I was going to leave the library alone today without at least talking to the pretty nun. When she stood up from her chair ten minutes later and walked toward the stacks to return her library book, I quickly collected my belongings and followed her. A dribble of lubrication run down the inside of my thigh as my pussy pulsed in excitement, knowing I was about to have my first real contact with the blue-eyed beauty.

3

____

SISTERS

When I entered the row where I saw the nun go to return her book, she was bending forward squinting at the call numbers on the spines of the shelved books. I stepped forward and tilted my head down slightly, smiling at her.

"You know you don't actually have to reshelve library books when you're finished with them," I said.

She stood up, flushing in her cheeks when she recognized me.

"Oh—yes," she said, in a soft voice. "I just figured the librarians can use all the help they can get. There's so few of them looking after such a big place."

My heart raced as I listened to her talk. She was even more beautiful up close than I imagined. She had flawless unblemished skin, and her azure-blue eyes penetrated me like a laser, deep into my soul. Completing the angelic imagery, her melodious voice reminded me of the virtual assistant on my phone, lulling me with its lilt.

I glanced at some of the book titles on the shelf in front of her and the category banner at the side of the stack.

"You're a fan of historical fiction?" I said, trying to break the tension.

The nun glanced at the marker, then smiled as she turned her book cover around for me to see.

"Not usually. Normally I stick to scripture and other Christian themes. But the title of this one intrigued me."

"*Jesus and the Riddle of the Dead Sea Scrolls*," I said, reading the title of her book. "That certainly sounds like it qualifies."

"I think its miscategorized. It's really more of a critique of the Bible, suggesting that the Dead Sea Scrolls offer a somewhat different explanation for the events surrounding the time of Jesus."

"Sounds interesting," I nodded. "What was your impression of the book?"

"I...kind of lost interest after the first few pages," the nun hesitated, looking away. "I guess it didn't exactly fit in with my world view."

She looked at the laptop bag slung around my shoulder and peered back at me with her piercing eyes.

"How about you? What were you reading today?"

"Oh," I said, momentarily caught off guard. "I wasn't actually reading anything specific today. I just like to come here every now and then to find a quiet place to work on some...personal projects."

The nun turned to face me directly, holding her book over her breast like a schoolgirl.

"What kind of work do you do?"

"Freelance graphic design mostly. Book covers, ad copy, corporate logos, that sort of thing." I looked at the pretty nun's smock and frowned. "Pretty superficial stuff compared to your life's work, I would imagine."

"You mean *this*?" she chuckled, pinching her gown and pulling it away from her body a few inches. "I think most people imagine the life of a nun to be one of the most boring vocations possible for a young woman."

"I wouldn't exactly choose that word. I imagine you have plenty of spiritual and emotional stimulation in your chosen field."

The nun nodded gently and sighed.

"Yes, there's plenty of that. Perhaps not as much intellectual stimulation as in your field, though. That's part of the reason I like to come to the library. There are lots of other—*perspectives*—to be found here."

Now I was the one who could feel a blush spreading over my cheeks. I paused, wondering how I could steal a few more private moments with her.

"I'd love to learn more about your life. It's all so mysterious. Do you have time for a coffee? You could enlighten me on spiritual matters, and I could regale you with all the fascinating logos I've worked on."

The nun chuckled, then paused to contemplate my offer.

"I'm not sure you'll find the life of a cloistered nun terribly interesting. I'm sure you have a far more fascinating life. Coffee might be breaking the rules though. I'll be happy to share some fruit juice with you."

I smiled, beginning to realize how pure and unspoiled she was.

"Fruit juice it is. I know a quiet spot not too far from here."

I extended my right hand slowly.

"I'm Jade."

The nun extended her hand and clasped mine softly in hers. My heart thumped in my chest, sending a surge of hormones racing to my pussy.

"Sister Caroline," the nun said.

"Should I address you as Sister, Caroline, or Sister Caroline?" I asked, unsure of the proper protocol.

"Sister is fine."

"Pleasure to meet you, Sister. May I offer you a ride to the coffee shop?"

"Sure. It's got to be more comfortable than the two buses I took to get here."

The pretty nun and I continued making small talk on the way to the coffee shop, with neither one of us broaching the subject of what had happened between the two of us earlier at the library. When we got to the coffeehouse, I ordered two fruit juices and we found a quiet corner of the shop near the fireplace with two upholstered chairs.

"This is a cozy little spot," the nun said. She closed her eyes and took a deep breath through her nostrils. "And the smell is divine."

"I thought you didn't like coffee?"

"This aroma is bringing back the memories. After taking my vows, I gave up a *lot* of little pleasures I'd almost forgotten."

We paused for a long moment smiling at one another, then the nun took a sip of her juice.

"Do you mind my asking what kind of vows you've taken?" I asked. "I'm ashamed to admit that all I know about nuns is what I saw in the movie The Sound of Music."

"We could do worse than that in terms of public perception," the nun chuckled. "That was another one of my favorite things from my previous life, to steal a phrase. I always admired Julie Andrews. I think her depiction of a nun's life is partially what drew me to it."

My eyes crinkled, recognizing a common bond. I was rapidly developing more than just sexual feelings for Sister Caroline.

"You know you look a little bit like her," I said. "The same piercing blue eyes, soft pretty features..."

"You're far too kind, Jade. But to answer your question, we take three separate vows for poverty, chastity, and obedience."

"Obedience in terms of adhering to scripture?"

"Actually, the obedience part pertains to our promising to follow the rules of the abbey and the guidance of our abbess."

"Abbess?"

Sister Caroline chuckled.

"That's mother superior, to our Sounds of Music fans."

"And the poverty part? Is that why you can't drink coffee?"

"That wouldn't be breaking the rules, per se. But we're expected to follow a life of austerity once we enter the abbey. The menu at the abbey is kind of bland, but you get used to it pretty quickly."

I paused, unsure how to broach the delicate third subject.

"And the chastity part? Was that something that you had trouble adjusting to also?"

"At first, no. We actually go through a ceremony where we're literally betrothed to Jesus. Once the temptations are removed in the sheltered confines of the abbey, you soon learn to not think about the temptations of the flesh any longer."

"And when you *leave* the abbey?" I said, finally addressing the elephant in the room. "How do you manage the temptations then?"

"I was doing fine," she said. "Until I saw you."

I paused, looking into the nun's eyes with a pained look on my face.

"Sister..."

"I think perhaps you should call me Caroline. It feels a little strange under the circumstances you calling me sister."

"I agree," I said. "Caroline. I like that name. It's soft and pretty—like you."

"I was thinking the same about you, Jade. It's been hard for me to take my eyes off you. It wasn't just because..."

I leaned forward and placed my palm over Caroline's hand resting on her armchair.

"I'm sorry about being so forward," I said. "I couldn't resist. From the moment I first saw you, my body seems to have a mind of its own whenever I'm around you. And then when I saw you reacting to me the way you did—"

"Was it that obvious?" Caroline said.

"Not to anyone else in the library."

"I hope not. Otherwise, my abbey's switchboard will be flooded with calls from outraged Christians."

"You were very...*proper*," I chuckled. "I'm quite sure I was the only one who noticed that you were enjoying more than just your book in your chair."

"Not nearly as much as *you*," Caroline said, her cheeks flushing a deep shade of crimson. "It was a lot more—*obvious*—how much pleasure you were experiencing on the other side of the room."

Hearing Caroline acknowledge our sexual connection for the first time suddenly sent a flood of juices pouring out of my pussy. I crossed my legs, feeling the moisture coating the inside of my thighs.

"You have that—*effect* on me," I said. " I think I could have just as easily—*enjoyed myself*—just watching you. I barely even needed to touch myself."

Caroline smiled at me warmly, as I noticed her bosom begin to rise and fall in silent excitement.

"I'm glad you did though. You're beautiful—everywhere. When I first caught you squirming in your chair yesterday, it was like a different power overtook my body."

I squeezed my thighs together, pinching my clit between my legs.

"While you revisited another one of those earthly pleasures you'd almost forgotten?"

"Yes," Caroline said. "And not just once. I've revisited those pleasures several times since yesterday. You're a difficult image to shake from one's memory, Jade."

As I crossed my legs trying to contain my rising passion, I felt the juices pouring out of my opening, dribbling down the crack of my ass.

"So what do we do now?" I asked. "Keep meeting for clandestine rendezvous at our local public library? Sooner or later, someone's going to catch on to us."

"I think you're right," Caroline nodded. "We're both taking unnecessary risks."

I looked around the coffee shop and noticed many people suddenly turning away. It was apparent that the pretty nun in her black habit had become the center of everyone's attention.

"Why don't we go somewhere where there aren't so many prying eyes? I can make us some more fresh juice at my place. That is—if you don't need to get back to the abbey right away..."

"What time is it?" Caroline asked. "I don't have a watch."

I pulled my phone out of my purse and tapped the screen to wake it up.

"Ten fifteen."

"It's still early," she said. "I might not be missed until the afternoon communion..."

For the entire duration of the twenty-minute drive back to my place, Caroline and I didn't say a word to each other, the sexual tension was so thick between us in the car. As she looked out her passenger window watching the passing scenery, I squeezed my thighs together, trying to keep my throbbing pussy from completely soaking the underside of my skirt.

When we got to my house, I opened the front door and invited her in. She looked around my living room and nodded approvingly.

"You have a lovely home," she said. "Tasteful and understated, just I expected."

"I wouldn't have thought you'd expect anything *understated* about me after today," I laughed. "Come to the kitchen and let me see if I can fix you up something more to your liking."

I led Caroline to my open kitchen and offered her a bar stool at the large central island.

"What do you feel like?" I asked. "Water, juice—or maybe something a little stronger? I don't suppose you're allowed to partake in certain other types of spirits?"

"We do occasionally partake in communal wine," Caroline chuckled, "so long as it's been properly consecrated first. Hopefully I won't be struck down for drinking something other than the blood of Christ, this one time."

"White wine it is then," I said, pulling a bottle of chardonnay from my fridge. "We don't need any more judging eyes upon us today."

I placed two wine glasses on the counter and filled the goblets halfway, then sat down beside Caroline.

"To rekindling forgotten memories," I said, holding my glass in the air.

Caroline tapped her goblet gently against mine, then took a small sip from the glass.

"There's been one other thing I've been meaning to ask you," I said, peering up at her white headdress. "Why is your hood white? Don't most nuns wear a black veil?"

"You're not the only one who's asked me that," she said. "Nuns normally go through a period of testing when they first enter the religious order, called a postulancy. For the first couple of years, we wear a white veil, signifying that we're still novitiates, or novices. Once we pass this initial test, if the nun and the abbess agree that the monastic life is what they desire, we take our final vows and receive the traditional all-black habit."

"So you're still—*testing* the waters, then?"

"I suppose so. I'm getting pretty close to the end of my postulancy period. My mother superior will be expecting me to take my final vows soon..."

"Do you feel ready?"

Caroline paused for a long moment with a pained look on her face.

"I thought I was. Until I met you. Then suddenly, my thoughts were no longer so pure..."

I set my glass down on the counter and stared into Caroline's eyes, imagining how conflicted she must have felt at this moment. We paused for many long seconds peering at one another, then she leaned her face toward me unconsciously. I quickly closed the distance and placed my lips against hers gently. As she closed her eyes, she pressed her mouth harder against mine.

I swiveled my stool until I was facing her directly, then I brought my right knee forward, parting her legs. As Caroline's mouth opened, I felt her cool breath on my face. I pushed my tongue gently into her, tasting the sweet vestige of wine on her lips. Within seconds, we were holding each other in a passionate embrace, pressing our bodies tightly together over the bar stools.

"Jade," Caroline panted, pulling away momentarily.

I looked into her eyes, trying to divine her intentions.

"Caroline," I said. "Do you feel ready?" I repeated.

She peered through glistening eyes at me and paused for only a moment.

"Yes."

Then she leaned forward and closed her lips around mine.

4

UNCLOAKED

Caroline and I kissed awkwardly on the bar stools for a few moments, then I pulled away and suggested we go upstairs where we could be more comfortable. As I led her by the hand through the hall, I felt an electric charge running through my body knowing I'd soon see her disrobed. But when we got to my bedroom, I paused looking at her habit, unsure where to start.

"I feel a bit uncomfortable touching your gown," I said. "Somehow, it just feels—*blasphemous*. I don't know how..."

Caroline smiled softly at me, then reached her hands up behind her veil.

"I can see how it might seem a bit daunting," she said. "Let me show you how I take off my armor."

She turned around and reached under the pleated fold behind her hood, then removed a hidden safety pin holding the two sides together, closing the pin and placing it in her pocket. Then she flipped up the back of her veil and unclasped another safety pin holding the inner flaps together. Then she turned around and lifted her hood off her head. Underneath, she wore a white cotton headdress covering her ears, neck, and the rest of her head.

I stared at her as she disassembled her wardrobe, mesmerized by the multiple layers of strange regalia. She looked so pure and innocent bound up in her tight white hoodie.

"Is there somewhere I can keep my veil?" she said, holding the white hood in front of her.

"Yes," I said, hanging it delicately over the back of my chair so as not to wrinkle it.

When I returned, she had her hands behind her head, slowly untying some more connections.

"Can I help?" I said, frustrated by the slow pace of her undressing. "Two people might make this go a little faster."

Caroline chuckled then turned around. At the back of her head, I saw two cotton ties holding her headdress together.

"You weren't kidding about the body armor," I chuckled. "They've really got you all tied up in this thing, don't they?"

"It's not as bad as it looks," Caroline said. "It's actually quite comfortable. You get used to it pretty quickly."

I untied the cotton bows at the back of her headdress, then gasped. Her hair was shorn down to short stubs, revealing an almost bald head.

"Are you *sure* you want me to take this off?" Caroline said with her back still turned to me.

"Yes," I said. "More than ever." I looked at the back of her hoodie and saw some more clasps. "What now?"

"Remove the safety pin holding the flap at the back of my neck."

I reached up and found the pin and gently slid it out under the band.

"Good God," I said. "How do you manage to get all these pins in and out every day without stabbing yourself? Or do you just sleep in this thing?"

"Heavens, no," Caroline said. "We're expected to keep our habits in pristine condition. That would produce far too many wrinkles. I actually sleep in the nude most of the time."

My pussy pulsed at the thought of soon seeing her naked body.

"I'm dying to see you that way. How do we get the rest of this stuff off?"

"There's just one more pin to remove," she said. "At the bottom of my collar, you'll find another one holding the two flaps together."

I found the pin and removed it softly.

"Done."

Caroline turned around and smiled at me.

"Are you sure you're ready for this?" she asked.

"Yes," I said. "I want to see *all* of you."

Caroline reached behind her neck and removed her large oval collar and handed it to me. Then she reached behind her head and pulled her headdress forward off her head. When she showed her bare head for the first time, my eyes widened as big as saucers. Her baldness accentuated her soft features and beauty, reminding me of a young Sinead O'Connor.

"Caroline," I said. "You're stunning."

I leaned forward and kissed her on her lips and she pulled gently away.

"Don't forget about the wrinkling thing. I want to see you naked just as much as you do, but I've got to be presentable when I return to the abbey. Let's get the rest of these clothes off so we don't have to worry about it any longer."

She handed me the headdress and collar and I placed them flat on my work desk along with the pins. Now she stood before me wearing only her long black robe. The slow reveal was driving me crazy, and I could feel my pussy pulsing between my legs, anticipating what lay beneath.

Caroline threaded her fingers between the two sides of a long sash on the front of her gown, then pulled the strange garb over her head and handed it to me. Divest of the extra garment, I saw a long string of black prayer beads hanging down the side of her gown from her belt.

"This is called the scapular," she said.

"No wonder I couldn't make out your shape under your gown," I said. "How many layers do you have on this thing anyhow?"

"Just one more."

She reached around her back and unbuckled her belt, then handed it to me with the beads attached.

"Now the rosary..."

"Are you sure I won't get struck down by lightning touching this?" I joked.

"Let's hope not. But just to be safe, you might want to handle it by the belt only."

I held the belt out in front of me, being careful not to let the beads touch the ground, then laid it gently on my desk beside the other garments. When I returned, Caroline paused, looking at me unsteadily. I could tell she was a little nervous about revealing any more of her body.

"May I do this part?" I said, seeing the zipper running down the front of her tunic.

"Yes," she said, softly.

I slowly pulled the zipper down from under her chin and noticed that she wasn't wearing a bra.

"No undergarments?" I said, somewhat surprised.

"Not today," she said. "I wanted to feel...sexier. Normally, I wear an undershirt, bra, panties, and nylons. Something told me I might need to remove my habit a little faster today..."

I paused, realizing she was completely naked under this final layer. I stared into her eyes as I slowly pulled the zipper down. Listening to my heart pounding in my chest, I wasn't sure which one of us was more nervous. When the zipper reached the bottom of its travel, I pulled the upper halves of her tunic apart and peered down at her chest. When I saw her breasts, I gasped.

"Oh, God," I murmured.

Caroline's breasts were full and firm, standing in two perfect circles high on her chest. I reached in and cupped them with my hands and squeezed them gently, stepping forward and kissing her hard on her mouth. I could feel her chest rising and falling as she breathed heavily, blowing a soft breeze through her nostrils onto the sides of my cheeks. When I moved my thumb and forefinger over her nipples, I felt them harden, and she gasped in my mouth. As I rolled them gently between my fingers, she pressed her body firmly against mine.

We kissed for a few more seconds, then I moved my hands around the sides of her back, down toward her buttocks. As I ran my hands over her cheeks, they quivered in my hands and I pulled her toward me more tightly. When our mounds touched, we both let out a moan, and I felt Caroline's muscles contract in my hands as she pressed her mound against me.

"Jade," she panted. "This is all I've been able to think about. I want to make love to you."

She stepped back a couple of feet, then pulled her arms out of her sleeves and dropped her gown to the floor. When I saw her fully naked body for the first time, it took my breath away. She had a slender but shapely hourglass figure, with barely an ounce of fat anywhere on her body. Her whole body was white as fresh snow, except for a light brown triangle of pubic hair between her legs. I reached down and picked up her habit and folded it over the back of my chair, then returned to behold my pretty angel.

I stepped forward and ran my hands down the sides of her body, feeling the curvature of her hips, then I cupped her face in my hands and kissed her softly. Her body was shaking next to me, and as I touched her back, I felt goosebumps on her skin.

"Are you chilly?" I said.

"Maybe a little," she said. "I'm not used to being out of my habit for this long. Maybe I'm a little nervous too..."

"It's okay," I said. "We can take this slow. Let's get you under the covers where you'll be more comfortable."

I pulled the covers down from the edge of my headboard and gently sat Caroline on the side of my bed. Then I kneeled down on the floor between her legs and untied her black shoes and placed them beside my nightstand. With my face so close to her kitty, I could smell her sex wafting up from between her legs, and I wanted to pull myself into her so badly.

But I lay her down on the bed and pulled the sheets and comforter over her, then stood up. As she lay on my bed looking up at me innocently, I began to unbutton my blouse. Her eyes widened when she saw my full breasts pull away from my shirt, and I quickly pulled my arms out of my sleeves and threw my blouse on the floor.

"I'm not quite as worried about wrinkling as you are."

"Neither am I right now," she said. "Just get out of those clothes and get in here."

I quickly undid my skirt and dropped it to the floor. Even though Caroline had seen my naked vulva from across the library floor earlier, she was surprised to see my bare mound. Her eyes widened as she took in my body, squirming seductively under the covers.

"Now *you're* the one who looks pure and clean," she said, staring at the bare space between my legs.

I pulled off my shoes, then climbed in under the covers next to her.

"I'm sure I'm nowhere near as pure as you," I said, snuggling close to her. "But speaking of clean, I am feeling a little crusty from all the bodily discharges I produced watching you earlier today. Do you mind if I have a quick shower?"

Caroline wrapped her arms and legs around me and squiggled closer to me under the covers.

"Now?" she said. "You'd leave me to my own devices after teasing me so thoroughly?"

"Well if you don't think you can wait the five minutes it'll take me to clean up, you could always join me in the shower."

I turned around and opened my nightstand drawer.

"Or you could keep yourself amused with these other devices while I'm gone."

Caroline's eyes widened as she took in my collection of sex toys.

"Are those what I think they are?" she said.

"You've never used one?"

"Nothing quite so...elaborate. I've experimented using bottles and sundry pieces of fruit before, but these look a lot more —*sophisticated*."

I looked into Caroline's eyes and smiled a wide grin.

"You're in for a real treat then," I said. "But first, I want to have my *own* way with you before you get too attached to mechanical devices. Come, let's have a quick shower together to get cleaned up. It'll warm you up, too."

I threw the covers back then we scampered into my ensuite washroom, giggling like two little girls. I adjusted the water temperature in my shower until it was nice and warm, then I pulled Caroline under the spray. As the droplets bounced off her bald head and streamed down her face, I pulled her toward me and kissed her hard on her mouth. We rubbed our breasts together under the slippery water, clasping each other's buttocks, grinding our mounds against one another.

Caroline moaned gently, and I began to lower myself slowly down her body. As the water poured over me, I kissed her under her neck, tasting her sweet flesh. When I reached her chest, I paused to give each of her breasts plenty of attention, sucking and flicking her hardened nipples with my tongue, cupping and squeezing her tits between my two hands. The further I moved down her body, the more she moaned and whimpered, her stomach quivering in excitement from my touch.

It was obvious to me that she'd never been touched in this way by another person, and I savored every square inch of her magnificent, unspoiled body. When I got to her bush, I sucked the water droplets off her thatch like dew on the morning grass. Then I knelt down on the tiled floor, gently spread her legs, and kissed her pearl. Caroline gasped, grabbing the back of my head, and pulled me closer toward her.

"I thought you said we were going to get *clean* in here," she panted.

"That's exactly what I'm doing," I said. "I didn't say *how* we were going to get clean. Do you want me to stop?"

"God, no!" she said, pulling my head harder against her crotch.

When I slipped my tongue around her button and began to lather her with my serpent, Caroline threw her head back and moaned loudly.

"Yes, Jade," she whimpered. "Lick me. Lick me clean with your tongue."

Caroline's sexy comments surprised me, emboldening me to go further. I cupped her ass with my left hand and began trilling my fingers against her opening. Caroline bent her knees and tilted her hips, encouraging me to go further.

"Yes—take me," she said. "I want to feel you inside me."

I slipped my middle and forefinger into her cavern, and she pushed her hips down until my hand was buried inside her up to my knuckles. As she began humping her hips against my hand, I sucked her lengthening nub into my mouth.

"Oh God, yes," Caroline panted. "Suck me, Jade. It feels so good."

As her humping action increased in intensity, she pulled my head harder against her pussy. I could tell she was getting close, so I curled my fingers against her G-spot and flicked my tongue more rapidly over her rubbery clit. When I slipped my pinky finger further down her perineum and placed it over her anus, she gasped.

"Yes!" Caroline panted. "Jade, I'm going to—"

Suddenly, she emitted a guttural scream and pushed her muff hard into my face, as I felt her vagina and rosebud pulsing against my fingers. As she came into my mouth, I held her firmly in my hands, savoring her sweet nectar as the water streamed over my face.

"Jade—Jade—Jade!" Caroline panted with each pulse of her pussy. "I'm cumming! Oh—I'm cumming into your sweet mouth!"

It was odd to hear someone screaming in the throes of ecstasy without using any curse words, which just added to my excitement. As I felt the water streaming down over my ass and mound, my pussy quivered along with Caroline's. When she finally stopped shaking atop of me, I stood up and kissed her passionately, as the water streamed down over our faces.

Caroline wanted to return the favor, but I just wanted to get her back into bed as quickly as possible. I let her run the bar of soap over my body and between my legs, but I made sure to not get too worked up. There was so much more I wanted to do with her when we had the full and free roam of each other's bodies. When we were both thoroughly clean, we stepped out of the shower and toweled each other dry, then we scampered back into my bedroom and dove under the covers.

We kissed and intertwined our legs awkwardly for a few minutes, then I pulled myself away.

"Are you thoroughly warmed up now?" I said, looking into her eyes.

"Yes. You've practically brought me to a boil."

"Good," I said, throwing back the covers. "Because this is going to need a little more space."

Caroline pinched her eyebrows together and began to raise herself up.

"What did you have in mind? It's my turn to—"

I placed my hand on Caroline's chest and gently pushed her back onto the bed.

"It's okay," I said. "This is for *both* of us."

I lifted her knees off the bed then gently pressed her legs forward and apart until her thighs were resting on top of her chest. Then I moved my body forward and pressed my mound against hers.

"Uhnn!" Caroline grunted in surprise when our clits touched.

"Yes, Jade!" she said. "Make love to me."

She lifted her head and peered between her legs. Both of our buttons were hard and erect, protruding like little pencil erasers toward one another. I lowered myself slowly and swayed my hips over hers, watching out nubs bending and flexing in a playful little sword fight.

"Oh God," Caroline panted. "That feels so good! Stroke me, Jade. Rub me...*fuck* me!"

I widened my eyes and gasped at Caroline in mock astonishment.

"You dirty little girl," I said. "I sure hope no one else is listening right now. Otherwise you could be in a lot of trouble."

"So do I," Caroline said. "But right now it hardly matters. Take me. There's only one place I want to go right now."

I lay my body on top of Caroline's and began to grind my pussy into hers as we kissed passionately. For the first time, I felt her tongue press into my mouth, and we sucked and nibbled on each other as our hips gyrated together. I wanted to make this feeling last, but I was already so worked up from making Caroline cum earlier, I could feel my orgasm rising quickly within me.

I grunted into Caroline's mouth as my juices poured out of my cunt, coating her bush and thighs with my lubrication. I could feel myself getting close, and I pulled my face up so I could look at Caroline's face. As my mouth and eyes widened signaling my impending orgasm, Caroline suddenly began panting louder.

"Yes, Jade," she said. "*Cum* for me. I want to watch you cum all over me."

I lifted my body up in one last strain and thrust my pussy hard against hers.

"Caroline!" I screamed. "I'm cumming! I'm cumming in your sweet pussy!"

Caroline's pupils suddenly dilated and she called out my name.

"Fuck, yes!" she screamed with me. "I feel you! I'm cumming with you, Jade! Oh God—it feels so good!"

Suddenly, I felt a hard spray jetting up against my vulva as Caroline squirted her love juices into my opening. Feeling her cum against my pussy was too much. I swung my body around her and clamped our boxes together in a scissor position. I wanted to feel our pussies connected as we were cumming together.

"Uhnn—Caroline," I grunted. "Come in my pussy, baby! Fill me up with your sweet nectar!"

I pulled her leg up toward my chest, grinding our cunts together, feeling my contractions gripping my entire body. We jerked and heaved our bodies together for a full minute, watching the look of tortured ecstasy wash over our faces. When we were completely spent, I collapsed on the bed beside Caroline, panting and sweating. We lay beside one another for a long time, holding and caressing each other, then Caroline finally turned toward me.

"What time is it?" she asked.

My eyes widened and I shook my head.

"Oh no," I said. "You can't..."

"I have to," she said. "The abbess will begin to worry if I'm not back soon."

I looked at Caroline through glistening eyes.

"But I don't want to let you go. I wanted to feel you fall asleep in my arms."

I turned my head toward my nightstand, thinking of how I could entice her to stay a little longer.

"And besides, you haven't even tried any of my toys. I had a few special ones in mind for you. When can you come back?"

"I don't know if I can," Caroline said. "These library excursions were meant to be temporary. I'm supposed to stay within the abbey. That's the whole point of my vows—to abstain from worldly temptations."

"But I thought you hadn't decided yet? Hasn't this changed your thinking at all about continuing on your life of abstinence?"

"It has, but I'm not ready to give it all up just yet. I need a little more time to think—"

"Can I visit you at the abbey at least? I just need to see you. I can't just let you walk out of my life forever."

Caroline looked at me with a pained expression and shook her head.

"It's too dangerous. People will notice there's something different between us—"

I reflected back to the videos of the naked nuns I watched earlier in the day.

"Is there somewhere I could meet you then, where no one would notice? Can you ever leave the grounds temporarily?"

"Not really."

Caroline paused for a long moment.

"But—"

"Tell me," I said. "I'll do anything, as long as I can see you again."

"There might be one way," she said. "But it's very dangerous..."

"What? Tell me!"

"I might be able to sneak you into the abbey for a short time. There's a secret passageway that we're not supposed to know about. A few other novices and I occasionally use it to slip outside to go for a walk. But we'd have to do it at night, and we'd need to have a signal."

I paused for a moment, thinking how I could notify her when I was near.

"How about if I hoot like an owl? There's plenty of those around here. Will you be able to hear it from inside the abbey?"

"I'll keep my window open," Caroline nodded. "But not tonight. The abbess will be watching too closely. Let's do it tomorrow night, just after dusk. Hoot three times in succession, so I know it's you. But be sure to do it convincingly, so it sounds like a real owl. I'll meet you at the south gate at the edge of the forest."

"I'll watch YouTube videos and practice all day," I said. "Will I be able to stay the night? I want to feel you in my arms when I fall asleep."

"Possibly. But you'll have to stay holed up in my room until the following night. Then you'll have to leave. It will be too dangerous for you to stay more than one day."

"I promise," I said, feeling my heart beating again in excitement. " Even one more day with you will feel like a lifetime. I just hope you'll reconsider your vows so we can see each other again. I don't want to lose you."

Caroline turned her body to face me and kissed me softly.

"You're so sweet, Jade. If anything could pull me away from the ascetic life, it's you."

Then she paused as she smiled into my eyes.

"And bring some of your toys. That might help."

MOTHER SUPERIOR

The next twenty-four hours seemed like an eternity, as I waited to see Caroline again. All I could think about was her radiant face and her pale, supple skin pressed against my body. I'd gone online and practiced my owl imitation as promised, standing in front of my mirror contorting my face and vocal chords, until I thought I'd gotten the pitch just right. As long as nobody saw me huddled in the surrounding woodland, I was confident I'd be able to pull it off.

An hour before dusk, I collected my belongings and drove north toward the remote address Caroline had given me. When I got to the monastery, there was a long drive leading up a hill, protected by a wrought-iron gate. I parked my car on a side street and tried to find a pedestrian access point, but the entire estate was surrounded by a tall iron fence topped with pointed finials, with locked gates all around.

Caroline had warned me about the barricade, so I removed a heavily padded blanket from my tote bag and flung it atop the spikes. I threw my purse over the fence then awkwardly pulled myself up the front of the fence and swung my legs over the top. I could feel the finials poking through the blanket into my stomach and chest, and swung my legs over the other side and fell onto the manicured lawn on the other side.

"These guys don't fool around," I murmured, feeling like a cat burglar invading a hallowed ground.

I made my way up the hill, trying to stay under the cover of the many mature trees scattered over the estate. When I got to the top of the hill, I saw a tall, steepled church flanked by two four-story block buildings. Caroline told me she was in the west residence, so I moved to that side of the compound and waited about thirty feet behind the rear entrance under a large elm tree. There was no sign of any activity on the grounds, which just added to the spookiness of the scene.

What the hell have I gotten myself into? I thought, looking around the quiet estate. *If anybody sees me, I'll stick out like a sore thumb.*

I'd worn special clothing to not be too conspicuous, and with my long dark pants, black sneakers, and black turtleneck, it just added to the cat burglar mystique. As the light dimmed over the estate, bats began darting over the dark sky and I heard rustling in the branches overhead.

This place is creepy, I thought, wondering if this was an omen of bad things to come.

But as dusk fell, I began to hear the familiar hooting of owls in the surrounding woodland, and as I listened to their calls I prepared to alert Caroline. At precisely nine-fifteen, I let out my signal.

"Hoo—hoo—hoo," I called out in my best falsetto.

Within seconds, a nearby owl returned my call.

"Hoo—hoo—hoo," I repeated.

Almost immediately, the owl hooted back.

If I can trick a real owl, I thought, *hopefully I can blend in with the rest of the local fauna.*

I waited five minutes, watching the back door to Caroline's building, but there was no sign of movement.

Had her abbess suspected something different about Caroline when she returned to the abbey and was keeping a closer eye on her? What if she can't get away?

I repeated my owl signal two more times, then I saw the back door swing open a few inches and Caroline stuck her head out, motioning for me to come in. I looked around to make sure the way was clear, then I scampered toward the door and jumped inside. Caroline and I kissed for a moment, then she pulled away with wide eyes.

"Jeesh—" she said, "do you think you could have made more of a racket out there? You've probably woken up the entire western wing!"

"It wasn't just me," I protested. "Apparently, there was another amorous owl out there competing for my affections. We had quite a little conversation going on for a while there."

Caroline giggled, then pulled a folded habit from under her cape and handed it to me.

"What do you want me to do with this?" I asked.

"We're going to need to disguise you, in case we run into anyone. It's only three floors and a short walk to my dorm, but I don't want to take any chances."

"Oh my God!" I said. "As if we haven't already broken enough rules. Now you want me to pretend I'm a *nun*?! God will surely strike me down before I get to your room."

"I'm sure he'll understand, under the circumstances," Caroline said. She removed the long tunic component from the pile. "Put this on first. Do you remember how it goes?"

"I've replayed your undressing ceremony in my head only about a hundred times since you left," I chuckled.

I stepped into the toga, then pulled the sleeves over my arms and zipped up the front.

"Good," Caroline said. "Now for the scapular."

She handed me the long flap draped over the front and back of the habit, and I pulled it over my head.

"Now the guimpe..." she said, handing me the large white collar.

She placed it around my neck and fastened it with the safety pin behind my back.

"Almost done," she said, handing me the white headdress. "Do you remember how to put on the wimple?"

"Of course," I said, placing my face through the hole in the front, then pulling it up under my chin and over my head.

"We won't worry about tying it at the back," Caroline said. "We haven't got far to go. It should hold until you get to my room. Now for the veil."

She lifted a black hood from my hands and placed it over my headdress, fastening it with two velcro tabs on top of my head.

"Why do I get a black one?" I asked.

"You're going to be a fully professed nun for tonight," she said. "You'll attract less attention this way."

"No prayer beads?" I joked.

"Let's not push it," she said. "You're already living on borrowed time as it is."

Caroline paused, as she looked at me approvingly.

"You know, you look quite suitable in a habit. Are you sure you don't want to consider joining our monastery full time? At least we'd have a chance to be together more—"

"I don't think I could manage the chastity part of your vows very well," I kidded.

"What now?" I said, looking up the stairs.

"Follow close behind me," Caroline said. "If we encounter any other sisters along the way, just keep your head down. Hopefully, nobody will recognize that you're an outsider."

"And if I am?"

"Well improvise."

"Is that where the lightning comes in?"

"Quite possibly."

I shook my head as I followed Caroline up the three flights of stairs, then she opened the door leading to her floor's hall and peered through the crack.

"All clear," she said. "Remember—stay close behind me."

I paused, reaching out to grab her arm.

"Shouldn't the more senior nun lead the way? Won't it look unusual for me to be following you?"

"Don't let that uniform go to your head, my lady. Just follow my instructions and we should be fine."

Caroline swung the door open and stepped out into the hall, then began walking down the corridor with her hands embedded under the sides of her gown. I mimicked her movement, holding my purse tightly against my abdomen, walking three feet directly behind. When we were about halfway down the hall, another nun suddenly turned the corner about a hundred feet ahead of us and began walking in our direction.

My heart raced in fear thinking I'd be detected, and I scurried up closer behind Caroline.

"What do we do now?" I whispered. "Surely she'll recognize that I'm not part of the congregation!"

"Just be calm and keep your head down," Caroline said.

I lowered my head, feeling my loose headdress falling down over my eyebrows, and I lifted my hand to push it back. After we'd closed the distance to about fifty feet, the nun stopped and turned to one of the residence doors and nodded gently toward us. Caroline returned the gesture, then the nun entered the room and closed the door behind her. Twenty feet ahead, Caroline stopped outside another door on the opposite side of the hall and quickly pulled it open motioning me inside. I scampered into her room, and after Caroline checked both ends of the hall to be sure no one else was watching, she slipped in and closed the door behind her.

We giggled quietly, then I pressed her body against the door and kissed her passionately on her lips.

"That was a close one," I said. "Do you think the other nun suspected anything?"

"I don't think so, but just to be extra careful we're going to have to be super-quiet as long as you're in my room. The horarium has ended for the day, so we've got the rest of the night to ourselves."

I leaned in toward Caroline and slipped my knee between her legs, pressing my thigh against her crotch as I kissed her. After a few seconds, she stepped away, pinching her eyebrows.

"Wrinkles!" she said.

"You've *got* to be kidding me," I said. "Don't you have an iron? They must provide *some* appliances to make your life easier—"

"We do. But it will just be easier if we get out of these clothes. Besides, I've been dying to see you naked again ever since yesterday."

"You don't have to ask me twice," I said, eager to get out of my religious garb as soon as possible.

We helped each other remove our garments, then Caroline hung and placed everything carefully in her wardrobe closet. When we were both naked, we pressed our bodies together, mashing our breasts and mounds against one another, kissing passionately. I moaned unconsciously from the delirious feeling of holding her close to me again, and Caroline pulled her face away, lifting her finger to her lips.

"Sh!" she said. "Not a peep. This place is like crickets at night. You can hear everything."

"That's easy for *you* to say," I whispered. "I don't know how I'm going to possibly contain myself around you."

"Well then, I guess you'll just have to do *me* first," Caroline smiled. "I've had more practice keeping quiet around here."

She looked at my large purse resting on the floor and widened her eyes.

"Did you bring some of your toys for me to play with?"

"I did," I said, smiling at Caroline mischievously.

I picked up my purse and placed it on her narrow bed, then pulled out a large purple dildo with a V-shaped extension near the base.

"This is one of my favorites. It's called a rabbit vibrator."

I pointed it up and turned the dial at the base of the dildo. The purple shaft began to vibrate and the tip of the dildo began to wobble in circles, as a ring of beads midway along the shaft began to rotate.

"Those don't look like prayer beads," Caroline said.

"No, but I think you might find them divine in an entirely different sense of the word."

Caroline looked at the animated device, widening her eyes.

"Do I put it *inside* me?"

"It works best that way. The oscillating head twists and turns, providing a heavenly form of stimulation against your G-spot."

"G-spot?"

"That the place inside you where I tickled you with my fingers yesterday."

"Oh yes—I remember that very well. That was the first time you took me over the edge."

Caroline placed her fingers over the strange rubbery protrusions on the side of the dildo. "What do *these* do?"

"Those are the rabbit ears. They provide direct stimulation to your clitoris while the shaft is pumping and churning inside you. The combined effect is really quite something."

"I can see how you were worried I'm might become too attached to these devices." She reached into my bag and pulled out a leather harness with a long red phallus attached to the front. "What about this one?"

"That's what's called a strap-on dildo. It's something I can use to—um—*make love* to you like a man."

"Do women *do* that to each other?" Caroline said, pinching her eyebrows together.

"Some do. It can actually be quite fun, when you're in the right mood."

Caroline glanced in my purse seeing a variety of other sex toys and shook her head.

"Where do we begin? You've brought so many—"

I pushed Caroline gently down on the bed and lay on top of her.

"First, I want to touch and feel you with my *own* body parts," I said. "I've been dreaming about tasting your sweet body for the past twenty-four hours."

I rubbed my tits against Caroline's and ground my pussy into hers, thrusting my tongue into her pliant mouth. As her breathing escalated, I began kissing my way down the front of her body toward her pussy. I played with her breasts for a few minutes, pinching and sucking her nipples, then I drew my tongue over her quivering tummy until I reached her pubic patch. I flapped my face over her soft bush, breathing her fresh scent deep into my nostrils.

The lower I went on her mound, the wetter her patch became until my face rested between her slickly coated thighs. When I placed my tongue over her clit and licked it like a lollypop, Caroline gasped. I looked up between her legs and she tilted her head down toward me.

"*Now* who's being the noisy one?" I said.

As we peered into one another's eyes, I took her jewel into my mouth and began dancing my tongue over her hard shaft. Caroline bit her lip and scrunched her eyes, trying to keep quiet. It was such a turn-on seeing her face contort in private pleasure as I nibbled on her fiery love button. Her mouth opened wider with her rising passion, and I placed my fingers at her opening, preparing to thrust them inside her. But she reached out and placed her hands over mine, stopping me.

"Wait," she panted. "I want to feel you...*fuck* me...if you're going to be inside me. Can we try your strap-on sex toy?"

I lifted my head and smiled at Caroline like a Cheshire Cat.

"I thought you'd never ask," I said.

I quickly got up off the bed and wrapped the leather harness around my hips then rocked my hips in the air, flapping the big phallus sticking out from my mound.

"Is that what a *real* man's penis looks like?" Caroline asked, wide-eyed.

"More or less," I said. "This might be a little larger than most, and it has a few extra features distinguishing it from a regular cock."

I tapped a button on the side of my belt and the penis suddenly began bouncing and oscillating from side to side. Caroline's eyes grew even larger, and she tilted her hips up toward me.

"Yes, Jade," she purred. "Fuck me with your big man cock. I want to feel you inside me."

My pussy pulsed and I felt a dribble of lubrication run down the inside of thighs. I ran my hand over the slick patch then rubbed it over the top of my phallus, simulating a masturbation effect.

"Mmm," Caroline said. "I think it will feel even better *inside* me. Stop playing with your cock and put it inside me."

Caroline's dirty talk was getting me even more turned on, and I kneeled on the bed between her legs and placed the tip of my artificial cock over her opening. I rubbed it up and down her slit for a few seconds then I pressed the head against her clit. She rocked her hips forward to provide more friction against her love button and moaned softly. I looked into her soft blue eyes then grabbed her hips on both sides and slowly inserted the cock into her cunny.

"Oh, God yes!" Caroline panted. "Fuck me with your big cock, Jade!"

I thrust my pole deep inside Caroline's pussy and began pulling her hips toward me as I fucked her harder. Her tits bounced up and down on her chest with each thrust of my hips, and she began swinging her head from side to side in pleasure.

"It feels so good, Jade!" she said, seemingly no longer concerned about how much noise she was making. "Fuck me harder. Make me cum all over your big cock!"

I could feel the base of the phallus rubbing against my own clit as I thrust in and out of Caroline, and before long I began to feel the familiar pangs of an orgasm rising within me. I reached to the side of my belt and pressed the vibrator button, suddenly feeling the device throbbing between my legs. I pushed my hips hard against Caroline's vulva, grinding the oscillating phallus against her clit.

"Oh God, Jade!" she panted. "You're going to make me cum! Here it comes—I'm cumming Jade!"

I looked down between her legs and saw her spraying all over my artificial dick as I pumped in and out of her. Feeling her love juices dripping down under my belt into my own pussy soon put me over the edge too.

"Caroline!" I panted, trying my best to keep my voice to a whisper. "Cum on me, sweetie. I feel you. Momma's coming with you!

I thrust my big dildo into Caroline's spasming pussy for a full thirty seconds, then I fell on top of her, kissing her passionately while I continued to pump my cock into her, savoring the slippery wetness between both of our legs. After a few minutes, I pulled out and lay beside her, kissing her face and neck softly.

"That was incredible," Caroline panted, looking into my eyes. "Those toys really *are* addictive, aren't they?"

"They can be. That's why I like to use them in moderation. There's still nothing quite like the natural feeling of skin on skin."

"Mmmm, I agree," Caroline purred. "Speaking of which, I think it's *your* turn for some good old-fashioned skin-on-skin lovemaking. What can I do for you now?"

"Well, now that you mention it, there *was* something I had in mind.."

I removed my harness and placed the strap-on dildo on the corner of the bed, then swung my legs over Caroline's midsection and shimmied my hips up toward her head. When I got to her shoulders, I lifted my legs and placed my knees on opposite sides of her head. I paused for a moment, watching Caroline stare at my dripping wet pussy, then I slowly began to lower myself toward her face.

Just before I touched her lips, we heard a loud rapping noise on Caroline's door.

"Sister Caroline," an older woman's voice said from the other side of the door. "Is everything all right in there? I heard some unusual noises. May I come in?"

"Um—one minute, Mother Margaret," Caroline called back, her eyes wide as saucers.

She raised herself up off the bed and whispered for me to hide in the closet. Then she went to the wardrobe and opened the doors, putting on a terrycloth robe. I quickly picked up my purse and slipped inside, retreating to the far corner behind the hanging frocks. Caroline closed the door quietly behind me, and I peered between the narrow slats with frightened eyes. Caroline lifted her bedcovers and threw the rabbit vibrator and strap-on dildo under the sheets, then straightened her robe before heading to the door. I couldn't see her and the other nun from my vantage point, but I overheard the conversation clearly.

"Good evening, Mother," Caroline said. "Everything is fine. I was just preparing my bed to go down for the night."

There was a long pause, and I looked around Caroline's room to make sure all of my belongings were out of sight. Fortunately, she'd had the presence of mind to hang my clothes in the closet, so for all intents and purposes, it looked like she was alone.

"May I come in for a moment?" Mother Margaret said. "I'd like to inspect your room to ensure everything is in order."

"Of course. But I don't think you'll find anything out of place. You know how neat and fastidious I am."

"I do," Margaret said. "This won't take long."

I heard some footsteps moving toward the closet, then a nun wearing an all-black habit passed by my door. I crouched lower under the hanging robes and held my breath so as not to be heard. The mother superior looked around Caroline's room and noticed a bump in her covers and bent over to smooth them with her hand. Her eyes widened when she felt a hard object under the covers, and she swung the covers down, revealing the rabbit vibrator.

"What's this?" she asked.

"It's a—" Caroline paused, trying to think of how she could explain the strange object, "...*massager*. It helps loosen up my tight muscles when I get cramps."

"*Really*?" Margaret said, in a condescending tone. "You know most electric devices are banned from use in this abbey. But I might make an exception in this case, depending on your need. Show me how you use it."

Caroline looked at the mother superior in shock as her mouth tipped open.

"It's okay, my child. I merely want to see how it relieves your —*pain*."

Caroline picked up the vibrator by its purple shaft and twisted the control knob on the bottom. The vibrator began whirring and twisting in her hand, and she placed it against the back of her neck, turning her head from side to side, simulating the relaxation of her shoulder muscles.

"That's quite an interesting device," Margaret said. "May I see it for a moment?'

Caroline hesitated, then turned the vibrator off and handed it to her superior.

Margaret held it up in her hands for a moment and twisted it around in her hands.

"Why is it shaped like a *penis*, I wonder?" she said. She ran her hands over the tip of the phallus. "It appears to be anatomically correct—except for these strange flaps on the side. Where *else* have you been placing this massager to relieve your pain?"

It was obvious to me that Mother Margaret knew full well how the sex toy was designed to be used and that she was enjoying watching Caroline squirm as she tried to explain why she had it in her possession.

"Just my shoulders and back, mostly," Caroline said.

"*Mostly*?" Margaret said. "Show me. Take off your robe and lie down on your bed and show me how you use this thing to stimulate your muscles elsewhere on your body."

Caroline froze as she looked at the mother superior with a terrified look in her eyes.

"Go on, child. I'm *ordering* you. By your vows, you must follow all of my instructions. Let me help you off with your robe."

Mother Margaret stepped behind Caroline's back and pulled her robe off her body, then threw it on the base of the bed.

"Please continue, Caroline," she said. "Lie down on your bed and place that massager where it is designed to go."

Caroline lay down tentatively on the bed and began to rub the dildo over the sides of her body.

"*Lower*, my child. I think it's meant to go lower."

Caroline traced the vibrator down the side of her body until it rested on the side of her hips, then she pushed it into the sides of her buttocks, pretending to massage her hip muscles.

"Now, bring it—*inside*," Margaret instructed. "Between your legs. Place the purple penis between your legs."

Caroline paused for a moment, and the mother superior nodded for her to continue. She pulled the vibrator over her thigh and placed it awkwardly between her legs, rubbing it up and down softly over her slit.

"Yes, my child. Doesn't that feel better than using it to massage your neck or shoulders? Now, I want you to turn it on."

Caroline lifted the dildo above her hips and turned the dial part way. The vibrator began humming softly.

"*All* the way," Mother Margaret said.

Caroline twisted the dial clockwise until it wouldn't go any further. Suddenly, the penis became fully animated, twisting and oscillating noisily in her hand.

"Now place it between your legs, and let's see how pleasurable this massager can really be."

Caroline placed the tip of the humming vibrator at her opening and gasped.

"Does that feel better, Caroline?" Margaret said. "Is this massager relieving your stress in your nether regions?"

"Yes," Caroline panted.

"I think it's designed to massage your *insides* too," Margaret said. "I want to see you insert it into your private area. You've had far too much stress built up these past few months. Let's see if this special massager might relieve you of some of your burden."

Caroline paused for a moment, then inserted the tip of the vibrator into her slit. I could see the oscillating head turning and dancing over her opening, tickling her clit. As her long eyelashes fluttered in obvious pleasure, I couldn't help reaching down between my own legs to play with my own clit. There was something incredibly sexy about watching her masturbate herself while being watched by such an austere authority figure.

"*Deeper*, my child," Margaret said. "Press it deeper inside you. Feel the phallus filling you up, massaging your deepest regions. Relax and enjoy the stimulation of your special massager."

As Caroline inserted the dildo deeper into her pussy, I could see the rabbit ears flapping along the side. When she pressed the ears directly against her clit with the oscillating dildo embedded all the way inside her, she grunted loudly.

"Yes, Caroline," Margaret said. "Doesn't that feel better? Is that relaxing all of your muscles now?"

"Yes, Mother," Caroline panted, beginning to hump her hips, thrusting the vibrator in and out of her. "It feels...very good."

"Continue, my child," Margaret beseeched her. "Continue massaging your inner regions to see if you can relieve *all* of your stress."

"Yes Mother," Caroline panted, beginning to lift her hips off the bed as she hammered the dildo in and out of her.

It was the sexiest thing I may have ever witnessed, and I bit my lip trying to stifle my moans as my juices poured over my hand trilling between my legs.

"Oh Mother," Caroline said. "I can feel it—beginning to—ease my pain. It feels very good."

"Yes, my child. Push it harder up inside you. Make sure it reaches all of your sore muscles."

Caroline lifted her hips high over the bed and pulled the vibrator as far into her as she could, holding the vibrating ears tight against her mound. I could see the wings flapping wildly against her clit as she opened her mouth at the height of ecstasy. Suddenly, she grunted loudly and began shaking her hips uncontrollably.

"Uhnnn!" she grunted. "Oh God, I feel it, Mother!"

"Yes, my child," Margaret said. "Feel his blessing sweeping over you. You are truly filled with the spirit of Jesus."

Watching Caroline cumming so hard in front of the mother superior unfurled my taps, and I gushed all over my hand as my pussy clamped down over my fingers. It took a superhuman effort to not utter a sound, as I jerked silently in the darkness of the closet.

Caroline held her hips up in the air as she spasmed in a long and sustained orgasm for many seconds. When the wave finally passed, she flopped back on the bed, panting heavily.

"There now," Margaret said. "Doesn't that feel much better?

Perhaps we can find a good use for this automated stress-reliever after all."

Margaret kneeled on the bed and took the dildo out of Caroline's pussy and inserted it into her mouth, sucking her juices seductively from the shaft.

"I've been feeling some built-up stress of my *own* lately..."

As she knelt on the base of Caroline's bed and began to lift the front of her habit, she suddenly paused and ran her fingers over the covers. Feeling something else under the covers, she pulled them back all the way, revealing the strap-on dildo.

"What have we here?" she said, looking at Caroline mischievously. "Have you been using these special massagers with some of our other sisters? I think perhaps it's time I reminded you who's *really* in charge around here."

As she began to remove her habit, Caroline glanced toward the closet doors. I wasn't sure if she could see me peering back at her, but I sure as hell could see her and the mother superior vividly. And I was about to get the show of a lifetime from my dark little peephole...

VOLUME FOUR

THE EXCHANGE STUDENT

1

———

I almost missed the ad while rushing out of the grocery store after a long day of work. Tucked away in a corner of the bulletin board near the exit door was a small poster with the headline *Earn Extra Income Hosting a Foreign Exchange Student*. I paused for a moment, then pulled my cart closer to the board to read the message:

Earn money while helping a foreign student expand their cultural horizons. There's no better way to learn a new language and appreciate other cultures than to live with someone from another part of the world. By hosting a young person from a different country, you promote friendship, understanding, and cooperation in your home and community. Welcome a foreign exchange student into your home today and open the door to an exciting new world of experiences. Contact exchangehost.com for more info.

After reading the ad, I suddenly became aware of how hard my heart was pounding in my chest. I'd lived alone after separating from my husband more than two years ago, and my big house had become far too quiet and lonely. Having never had children of my own, the idea of hosting a young person from another country seemed a perfect fit. I'd have someone to liven up my daily routine while helping the student develop a sense of independence in an exciting new environment.

When I got home, I went to the agency's website and read everything I could about the program. The more I learned, the more excited I became. I wasn't interested in the small monthly stipend I'd earn hosting the student so much as the sense of adventure taking in a boarder from a different country. It would be an opportunity to share cultural experiences, improve my foreign language skills, and make new friendships.

The following morning, I called first thing to book an appointment for an interview. When I got to their office, the receptionist escorted me into the director's suite where a smartly dressed woman in her fifties invited me to make myself comfortable while she took a seat in the opposite armchair.

"Welcome, Ms. Robertson," she said. "My name is Elise Laurent, the director of Exchange Host student exchange services. What brings you to our office today?"

"I'm interested in hosting a foreign exchange student," I said.

"I see you're here by yourself. Do you live alone?"

"Yes," I said, crossing my legs defensively. "Do you accept applications from single women?"

"Of course," she said. "It all depends on the individual's circumstances and motivation. Our primary concern is finding a safe and supportive environment for our clients. May I ask what attracts you to our program?"

"I saw an ad for your services at the supermarket. I've never had any children, and I like the idea of helping a young person supplement their education in a different country. With so much conflict and misunderstanding between countries and cultures, this seems an ideal way to foster better communication and friendship."

"You seem primarily focused on the benefits to the *student*," the director nodded. "What advantages do you see for you, personally?"

"It's not about the money, if that's what you mean. I'd do it for free, if that were an option. I live alone and work from home, so I have limited opportunity for social interaction. To be honest, I think it would be fun to have someone else to share my house with. Especially a young person who I could foster and take under my wing. I could take her shopping, go out to restaurants, visit national parks–it could be fun for both of us."

"So you're looking to host a female student only?"

"Not necessarily. I'd consider either gender, but I think it would be more fun hosting a girl."

The director nodded, scribbling some notes on a notepad.

"You say money isn't a consideration. May I ask what you do for a living?"

"I'm a freelance graphic artist. I help develop ads, logos, websites, and media campaigns for corporate clients."

"Do you own your home?"

"I guess technically the bank owns it until the mortgage is paid off," I chuckled. "But yes, I'm the sole title owner."

"Umm," the director hummed, scribbling some more notes. "Do you have an extra room and bath available for another occupant?"

"Yes," I said. "Frankly, that's another reason I'm considering this. My house is far too large for one person. I'll feel better making better use of the extra space and helping the environment by wasting less."

"Um-hmm," the Ms. Laurent nodded. "And you feel you'll have enough free time away from your work and other responsibilities to give your charge proper attention and care? It's not like taking in a boarder–these students will need oversight and companionship. They'll be a long way from home in a whole new environment. It's more akin to a foster parent situation."

"Absolutely," I said. "Being self-employed means I can make my own hours and work around my guest's schedule. I'm looking forward to taking her under my wing and making a new friend. Like I said, I'm not doing it for the money."

"Okay," the woman said, putting down her notepad. "We'll need you to fill in an application and provide three references. Then I'll need your approval to run a criminal record check and credit check. If everything pans out, we'll begin contacting you with possible candidates to find a good fit. The whole process can take two or three months and with a new school year approaching, you'll need to get started soon."

"Sounds good," I said, rising from my chair and extending my hand. "Thank you for your time and assistance, Ms. Laurent. I'll look forward to hearing back from you at your earliest opportunity. Let me know if you need any more information in the meantime."

"It's been my pleasure," she said. "Thank you for your interest in our program. I think you'll find this experience enriching and rewarding on both sides. My assistant will help you with the paperwork. We'll be in touch soon."

After filling in the application, I drove home with a sense of excitement wondering who the agency would find to connect me with. I had no idea what age, sex, or nationality the student would be and that was part of the attraction. It would be a whole new experience for both of us. But after a few weeks of not hearing from the agency, I began to wonder if they were having second thoughts about my candidacy. I'd checked with my references who told me they'd already been contacted, and I knew there wouldn't be any issues with my background or credit check, so with only a few weeks left before the start of the new school year, I placed a call to the director.

"Exchange Host," the receptionist said, answering the phone.

"May I speak with Ms. Laurent?" I said.

"May I ask who's calling?"

"My name is Jade Robertson. I had an interview with Ms. Laurent a couple of months ago and haven't heard back. I was just hoping for an update."

"One moment please," the receptionist said.

"Hello, Ms. Robertson," the director said when she picked up her extension.

"I'm sorry to bother you," I said. "But I haven't heard back from you and I know we're getting close to the start of another academic year. I was wondering if you had any problems with my application or if you'd vetted any potential candidates."

"No," the director said. "Your application came through with flying colors. Unfortunately, it was processed a bit late and all of the hosting spots for the new school year have been filled."

"That's disappointing to hear," I said. "So I guess I'll have to wait another year for consideration?"

"Not necessarily," she said. "We have a number of students who seek to transfer mid-year. There may be another opportunity as we approach the end of the first semester. We'll contact you if anything becomes available."

"Okay, thank you, Ms. Laurent."

I hung up, feeling dejected about prematurely getting my hopes up. The closer we'd gotten to the start of the school year, the more excited I'd become about having a new housemate. Now I'd have to wait a whole other year to have the opportunity to host a student.

For a while, I considered putting an ad in the local university newspaper offering a room for board, but I knew it wouldn't be the same. There was something about taking in a young international student that added an extra allure for me. I'd have the chance to nurture someone who really depended on me while we explored each other's language and culture. In the end, I decided to hold off, hoping to try again next year.

But much to my surprise, I received a message from Ms. Laurent a couple of months later indicating that she had a new candidate lined up for the spring semester. I picked up the phone and called her immediately.

"Hello, Ms. Laurent," I said excitedly when she picked up the phone. "It's Jade Robertson. I got your message regarding a possible candidate for the spring semester, and I'm still interested."

"That's wonderful news," she said. "We're ready to finalize the placement if you're sure you're ready to proceed."

"Absolutely," I said, still catching my breath.

"Would you like to view the student's profile before making a final commitment? We can send it to you via email if you prefer."

I paused for a moment, hearing my heart pounding in my chest. As eager as I was for more details, I couldn't wait for the most important information.

"That would be helpful, thank you," I said. "Can you tell me if it's a boy or a girl, and from which country they'll be transferring?"

"It's a girl who'll be completing the final semester for her senior year. She's transferring in from France."

France, I thought, feeling my heart skip a beat. I'd always wanted to travel there and learn to speak the language, but had never found the time. This would be my chance to learn more about their culture by experiencing it in a whole *different* way.

"That sounds exciting," I said. "When will she be arriving, and are there any final preparation requirements?"

"She's due to arrive January twenty-third, the weekend between first and second semester. The only other preparation requirement is a final in-home interview to ensure you have sufficient accommodation and resources to care for your guest. We can arrange a convenient time to visit next week if that will work for you."

"That's perfect. How about Wednesday at one p.m.? Thank you for keeping me in the queue for consideration with this placement."

"My pleasure, Ms. Robertson. I'll look forward to seeing you next Wednesday. Bye for now."

Later that day, I received the student profile via email. When I opened it, the first thing I saw was a single headshot photo. It was a bit grainy, but she looked pretty and fresh-faced, with wavy blonde hair and bright blue-green eyes. Her name was Luna, and she lived in Saint Denis, a suburb of Paris. She listed her hobbies as yoga, skiing, and dressmaking. Her father was an engineer and her mother was a nurse. She had two siblings, an older sister and a younger brother. Her career interests were international relations and fashion design.

Perfect, I thought. *We can exercise together, go skiing on weekends, and we both have an interest in women's fashion.* It sounded like a match made in heaven.

After successfully passing the home inspection and knowing I'd have a girl as my guest, I went about decorating her room like I was expecting a newborn baby. I went out and bought a new work desk and bookshelf at Ikea and new towels and linens from Bed, Bath, and Beyond. The closer I got to her arrival date, the more excited I became about having my new houseguest. For the next four or five months, I knew my life would never be the same.

2

———————

As Luna's arrival date approached, I busied myself tidying up her room, decorating it with girly stuff. I painted the walls pale blue, bought lots of pretty throw pillows, and hung a beautiful photo of the Eiffel Tower to remind her of home. I even picked up a basket of beauty products from the French store L'Occitane, including lavender-scented bubble bath, shea-butter soap, and cherry blossom shampoo and conditioner. I wanted to do everything I could to make her adjustment as smooth as possible.

When her arrival date finally came, I drove with Ms. Laurent from the placement agency to O'Hare airport. While we waited outside the International Arrivals lounge, I tapped my foot nervously, checking my watch every two minutes wondering what was holding her up.

"Shouldn't she be here by now?" I said to Ms. Laurent. "Her flight arrived more than an hour ago."

"This is normal for international arrivals," she said, holding a sign with Luna's name on it as passengers began steaming out of the terminal. "She still has to clear through immigration, pick up her checked bags at the baggage carousel, and find her way through this maze of an airport."

"Does she have your phone number in case she gets lost?"

"Yes, but I'm sure it won't come to that," she said, placing her hand on my forearm, trying to calm me down. "Don't worry, there's only one exit from her arrival terminal, and she was told that we'd be waiting with a sign."

I scanned the swarm of passengers exiting the baggage claim area, trying to recognize her face from the picture in her profile. After another fifteen minutes or so, I saw a young girl throw up her hand and move toward us. When she reached our position, she stood her roller bags on the floor and reached out her hand to Ms. Laurent.

"Madame Laurent?" she said with a lilting French accent.

"Bonjour, Luna," Ms. Laurent said with an equally strong accent. "Comment était votre vol?"

"C'était bien," the girl said, shaking her head in dismay. "Mais c'est un très grand aéroport!"

"Je suis désolé," Ms. Laurent replied. "Je suis content que tu ne t'es pas perdu."

Then the director turned to face me, extending her hand in my direction.

"May I introduce you to your American host, Ms. Jade Robertson?"

"Pleased to meet you, Ms. Robertson," the girl said in perfect English.

"Please, call me Jade," I said, shaking her hand softly as she bent her knees in a gentle curtsy.

I was immediately taken by how beautiful she was up close and in person. She had wavy blond hair with a tinge of red, falling softly over her emerald-green eyes and creamy skin. With her high cheekbones, gently upturned nose and plump, rosebud lips, she looked like a young fashion model straight out of Vogue magazine. Wearing a sheepskin-lined leather bomber jacket overtop skinny jeans and Converse sneakers, I could see how she'd already defined her own unique sense of style.

"Do you need to use the restroom or get something to eat?" Ms. Laurent asked the girl.

"I had a snack on the plane, thank you," she said. "And I found the *toilette* in the baggage claim area."

Even the way she pronounced everyday pedestrian words like toilet in her native tongue was charming. I was already swooning over her, and I'd only met her for a few minutes.

"Can we help you with your bags?" Ms. Laurent said.

"Yes, thank you," the girl said. "I'm really getting a workout juggling these three bags."

Ms. Laurent reached out for the large check bag and I grabbed the smaller carry-on roller while Luna hiked her large tote bag over her shoulder.

"Let's get you situated, then," Ms. Laurent said, pulling the large roller bag in the direction of the ground transportation exit door. "Our car isn't parked too far away."

We packed Luna's bags in the trunk of my car, and I invited her to sit in the front passenger seat while Ms. Laurent sat in the back. As we exited the parking garage and pulled onto the 294 ring road heading south, Luna peered out the side window at the passing cityscape of downtown Chicago.

"You live in a very tall city," she said, gazing at the skyscrapers with wide eyes.

"Yes, I suppose it is," I nodded. "But Paris is a large city too. Doesn't it have a lot of skyscrapers also?"

"Very few, and they're all outside the main city. The city planners banned tall buildings to preserve its unique European flavor. Except for the Eiffel Tower, of course."

"Paris sounds so beautiful," I nodded. "I really must go there soon."

"Perhaps I can return the favor and host you when you visit?" Luna said, peering over at me through long eyelashes.

"That would be lovely," I said, almost missing my exit heading west toward the Naperville suburbs.

"So you live outside the city also?" Luna asked.

"Yes, but I'm only about twenty miles or so from downtown."

"I'm not familiar with miles..."

"That's equivalent to about thirty kilometers," Ms. Laurent chimed in from the back seat.

"Sorry," I said, reaching over to clasp Luna's hand gently. "I'll have to get in the habit of speaking European."

"Not at all," she said. "I'm a guest in your country. It's better that I begin learning about your American culture right away."

When we pulled into my driveway, I removed Luna's bags from the trunk and she peered up at my two-story house.

"What a beautiful home you have, Ms. Roberts–I mean, Jade," she said. "Everything in America is so *big*!"

"Thank you," I smiled. "But this really is just a typical middle-class home here in Chicago. Hopefully, you'll find plenty of room to stretch out. Come, let me show you around."

I escorted Luna and Ms. Laurent through the front door into the foyer, then hung their coats in the closet. Luna was wearing a tight cashmere sweater that matched the color of her eyes, and it took every ounce of my willpower to keep my gaze focused above her prominent, pointy breasts sitting high on her chest. We walked down the hall toward the kitchen, and I placed her bags at the foot of the stairs to the second floor. When she noticed the covered pool in my backyard, she rushed toward the window excitedly.

"You have a *pool* also?" she said. "Ms. Laurent never mentioned that!"

"Unfortunately, it's not much use during the long winter months," I said. "Hopefully we can get it up and running before you head back home." Then I pointed to the hot tub resting in the corner by the exit door. "But I *do* have a Jacuzzi that's quite relaxing on a cold winter day."

"I feel like I'm staying at a luxury hotel," Luna said.

"I wouldn't go that far," I smiled. "But I'm glad you find the accommodations suitable so far."

Ms. Laurent placed her briefcase atop the kitchen island and flipped it open.

"Shall we go over the final arrangements?" she said. "I think it's time you two settled in and begin getting to know one another."

"Certainly," I said. "Why don't you make yourselves comfortable in the living room? Can I get either of you a cup of coffee or tea?"

"Tea will be fine, thank you," Ms. Laurent said.

"Milk and sugar?"

"A little bit of both, thank you."

"Luna?"

"I'll have mine plain, thank you."

Plain it is, I thought, beginning to make a mental note of her preferences. But everything about this girl screamed she was anything but plain.

After I prepared the tea, I brought the cups into the living room and sat down on the sofa next to Luna.

"I've already gone over the protocol with both of you at some length," Ms. Laurent said. "So I won't bore you with too many more details. I just wanted to reiterate to Luna that as your official stateside sponsor, if you have any questions or concerns at any time, feel free to reach out to me at the number I've provided. That applies equally to you, Ms. Robertson. If you have any questions about legal matters or if any issues arise, please don't hesitate to give me a call."

"I've gone over the care package many times," I said, smiling at Luna as she beamed at me with a slight flush in her cheeks. "Everything looks pretty straightforward. I'm sure Luna and I will get along famously."

Ms. Laurent had us sign the final releases, then she glanced at her phone as it buzzed softly on the coffee table.

"It looks like my taxi is here," she said. "I'll look forward to hearing how you're enjoying your new surroundings, Luna. We'll talk again soon."

After I escorted Ms. Laurent to the front door and watched her pull out of the driveway, I helped Luna carry her bags upstairs to the guest bedroom.

"This is your room," I said, placing her bags by the bed. "I've tried to decorate it with a light feminine touch and some accents from your home country."

Luna peered around the room and smiled when she saw the framed print of the Eiffel Tower.

"It's lovely," she said. "You needn't have gone to so much trouble."

"It's the least I could do for someone visiting America for the first time. Let me show you your bath."

I led her into the washroom across the hall from her room, opening the empty storage lockers.

"Although it isn't attached to your room directly, you'll have the exclusive use of this bathroom. I've cleared out all the cabinets and bought you some toiletries to get you started."

Luna picked up the scented soap in the basket and held it softly under her nose.

"You've gone to so much trouble for me already, Jade," she said, peering up at me through her thick locks of hair. "It's *already* beginning to feel like home."

"I'm glad," I smiled. "Why don't you unpack, then if you'd like, we can go to the supermarket together and get some food for dinner. Or would you prefer to go out to a restaurant?"

"There's no need to treat me any different than any other houseguest," she said. "How does that American expression go? I don't want to eat you out of house and home."

As I watched her bend over to peer inside the shower curtains, I couldn't help staring at her tight, heart-shaped ass.

God forgive me, I said to myself. *Remember, you're her guardian while she's away from home. Get your mind out of the gutter.*

There was something about this precocious French beauty that told me she was going to be much more than just an ordinary houseguest.

3
____

After Luna finished unpacking, we went to the supermarket together and picked up some food for dinner. I wanted to spoil her on her first day in the U.S., so I baked a prime rib roast with mashed potatoes and gravy, corn on the cob, and apple pie. We chatted about her interests and life experiences, and when I learned that she'd recently turned eighteen, I couldn't help seeing her in a whole new light. She seemed more mature than other girls her age, talking about how the move to a new country to finish out her last year of high school was driven by her desire for independence and to explore new opportunities.

The following day, we went shopping for school supplies, and I got her a new SIM card for her mobile phone so she could make local calls. It was a colder January than usual in Chicago, and when we got home, I invited her to join me in the hot tub. She hadn't packed a swimsuit, and knowing it was too early to invite her to go nude, I offered her my one-piece suit. We were roughly the same dress size, but her waist was definitely narrower and her breasts were firmer and pointier than mine. Before we lowered ourselves into the bubbling water, I admired her tight figure, feeling my pussy throb as the hot liquid enveloped my hips.

"Wow," Luna said, feeling the Jacuzzi jets swirling over her body under the churning water. "You weren't kidding about how relaxing this is. This feels heavenly."

"It's especially nice on a cold winter day," I nodded. "There's something about feeling the hot bubbling water with the cold surrounding air that makes it even more refreshing."

"That, and all these water jets caressing my body," she smiled. "It's like getting a massage from a hundred masseuses."

"You've never enjoyed a hot tub before?" I said, peering at the top of her breasts protruding above the surface of the water as the churning liquid swirled over her erect nipples.

"Not like *this*," she purred, resting her head against her seat rest. "I've had a Jacuzzi bath before, but never outside and never with another person."

I was tempted to tell her about the secret location in the tub where she could receive special stimulation on a different part of her body, but I figured I'd let her discover that for herself another day. It was still early in our relationship, and I didn't want to overstep my role as her host.

"So what do you think of America after your first two days?" I said, changing the subject.

"You mean besides how cold it is in the winter?" she chuckled.

"Sorry about that," I said. "Perhaps you should have looked to relocate to a warmer state like Florida or California."

"Something tells me I'm going to warm up to this place pretty quickly," she said, glancing down at my breasts bobbing atop the swirling water. "Besides, I kind of like the cold weather. My family takes frequent ski trips to the Swiss alps. I don't imagine there's much skiing in Florida or California."

"Florida, no. But you'd be surprised how many ski resorts there are in California. The Sierras get a fair amount of snow in the higher elevations."

"Are there any ski hills near Chicago?"

"There's a few resorts in northern Wisconsin about four hours from here. It's a far cry from the Swiss Alps, but they have passable trails for an intermediate skier."

"I never even thought about bringing my gear with me," Luna said, shaking her head.

"Do you prefer to ski or snowboard?"

"I'm proficient at both, but I'm a slightly better skier."

"Not to worry," I said. "We can rent some equipment at the slopes. Once you get settled in at your new school, we'll make a weekend excursion soon."

"I'd enjoy that very much," Luna nodded, adjusting her position under the swirling water.

"Are you nervous about moving to a new school tomorrow?" I asked.

"Not too much," she said. "I've managed to maintain fairly good grades, and the curriculum between the two school systems is pretty well aligned, so hopefully it won't be too much of any adjustment."

I noticed Luna spreading her arms out to her sides, searching for the new locations of the underwater jets. As she squirmed in her seat, I could tell she was curious to see what they might feel like on other parts of her body, but she was too shy to make such a bold move in my company.

"What about socially?" I asked, eager to see if she had a boyfriend. "Do you make new friends easily?"

"It usually takes me a while to form those kind of bonds," she frowned. "Transferring in the middle of the school year doesn't help."

"Well, I'm sure with your pretty looks and charming French accent that it won't take long for you to find new friends." Then I looked at her with an arched eyebrow and a slight curl of my lip. "Is there a special someone back home that you'll miss *especially* much?"

"Not really," Luna smiled, understanding my meaning immediately. "I've been so focused on my studies trying to make sure I get into a good university. I don't have any time for boyfriends."

My pussy twitched when I heard she was unattached. Suddenly, *I* was the one shifting uneasily under the churning water, desperate to feel the jets pulsing against my pussy as I peered at the pretty French girl.

Later that evening while Luna checked in with her family back home, I went to my bedroom and propped up my pillows, picking up a book from my nightstand. About a half hour later, I heard her run a bath, and I wondered why she needed to bathe again so soon after our long hot tub. Listening to the sound of her body rubbing against the metal tub while she lowered herself into the water, my mind soon drifted away from the book, imagining what she looked like naked.

I wondered if it was true what they said about French girls not shaving their private areas, and I couldn't stop picturing her pretty tits floating atop the clear water. As much as I enjoyed watching her undulate in the frothy water of the hot tub, I would have killed to be in the bathtub with her right now. After a few minutes, I heard a scraping sound like she was shaving her legs, and I smiled.

So much for European girls going au naturel, I thought. *Apparently, they're just as obsessed as American girls about maintaining their smooth skin.*

I found myself holding my breath as I strained to listen to the sound of the razor scraping her skin and the water sloshing over her naked body as she shifted her position periodically in the tub. After a while, the scraping sound stopped and for a while I couldn't hear anything in the washroom. Then I slowly began to hear the sound of ripples lapping against the side of the tub, and I wondered what she was doing. Straining to listen, I heard her begin to mew as the sound of rippling water began to escalate in pitch and frequency.

Is she...? I thought, suddenly sitting up in my bed.

As her breathing and soft moaning began to grow more notice-able, there was no longer any doubt. She was masturbating in the bathtub!

Now I knew why she wanted to take a bath so soon after our hot tub together. She'd apparently gotten just as aroused as me feeling the swirling water jets caressing her body, and she wanted to re-experience the feeling in the privacy of her own room. I wondered if part of it might *also* have to do with a similarly strong attraction she was feeling for me.

I tiptoed across my carpet and opened my door as wide as it would go, then ripped off my clothes, sitting spread-eagled on my bedspread. As I listened to her soft sighs and moans, I placed my fingers against my clit, surprised at how wet I'd gotten in the last few minutes. While the pleasurable sensations began to spread throughout my body, I closed my eyes imagining what she looked like as she touched herself in the bathtub.

Did she like to squeeze her tits like me when she played with her clit? Did she like to place two fingers inside her pussy and stimulate her G-spot while rubbing her palm against her vulva? Did she have one leg propped up on the side of the bathtub while she jilled herself spread-eagled in the sudsy water? I could almost see the flush spreading over her chest and cheeks as her pleasure escalated in intensity. It didn't take long for the image I was cultivating in my mind to get me so worked up that I experienced a sudden orgasm, squealing softly as I bit my lip.

Suddenly the sloshing sound in the bathroom stopped for a moment as Luna paused to hear what I was doing. While I lay on the bed motionless with my fingers still embedded in my pussy, I felt my heart pounding in my chest as I struggled to slow my breath so Luna wouldn't know what I'd been secretly doing while she touched herself. Then a few moments later, the rhythmic sloshing sound resumed and I heard her moaning and sighing as her body squeaked against the slippery metal surface of the tub.

This time, I remained perfectly still while I curled my fingers softly inside my pussy, listening to Luna's breathing and groans growing more pronounced. Suddenly, I heard a loud splash as she jerked her body forcefully in the tub, and I knew that she'd reached orgasm. Consumed with desire, I began pounding my fingers in and out of my pussy while I tribbed my burning clit with the fingers of my other hand.

This time, my orgasm washed over me like a freight train, and I arched my hips high off the bed, gaping my mouth wide open in the throes of a powerful climax. Trying to stifle my moans, I held my body in an arched position for almost thirty seconds as wave after wave of intense contractions rolled over my body. When I finally collapsed onto my bed, the springs squeaked loudly, and the house became eerily silent.

I wondered if Luna sensed that I'd been pleasuring myself while I listened to her, just as she'd done with me. Either way, something told me there'd be a lot more than just *studying* going on in my household over the next four or five months.

4

For the next few weeks, things quieted down as Luna settled in to her new school and concentrated on her studies. We went shopping on weekends, watched movies together on the sofa on weeknights, and enjoyed frequent hot tub dips. But as much as I sensed the burgeoning sexual tension between the two of us, neither of us felt brave enough to make the first move for fear of breaking our unwritten host-student pact.

With the mid-winter school break approaching, I asked Luna if she wanted to head north for a few days of skiing. When she quickly agreed, I booked three nights at a cozy hotel near Granite Peak at Rib Mountain State Park. Luna was an excellent skier, and I had a hard time keeping up with her down the mogul-covered expert trails. In the evenings, we went out for dinner at local restaurants and by the time we returned to the hotel, we were both so exhausted, we fell asleep before ten p.m. But I saw enough of her in her skimpy underwear to have vivid dreams fantasizing about pouncing on top of her on the adjacent bed in our single hotel room. By the time we headed back home, I felt our relationship had reached a new level of comfort and closeness.

"Did you enjoy our little getaway?" I said, peering over at Luna as she stared out her window on the drive home.

"Yes, thank you so much, Jade," she said, turning to face me with a big smile. "You're the best host I could have ever hoped for. Sometimes I feel like I've hardly left home. Between the ski trips, restaurants, shopping, and everything else, you've made me feel like part of your family."

"Everything but the *hot tubs*, right?" I grinned.

"I have to admit, that's a lovely perk," she nodded. "Although with the weather beginning to warm up, we might not have so much need for it soon."

"In another month or so we can look into opening up the pool. It's heated too, so maybe you'll find it just as relaxing and refreshing on cool evenings and weekends."

"I'll have to look into getting my own swim suit soon," she smiled. "I'm going to wear yours out pretty soon with all the use it gets in the hot tub."

"Now that you *mention* that," I said, peering over at her. "I've been thinking. You've told me about your dressmaking hobby and your interest in exploring fashion design as a potential career. I'd like to buy you a sewing machine so you'll have something else to do with your free time."

"I could never expect you to buy me such an expensive gift," Luna said, shaking her head. "You've already spent far too much paying for the hotel and the restaurants on this ski trip."

"Hey, I enjoyed those just as much as *you* did. Besides, I've been wanting to get a sewing machine for myself for some time now. They're not that expensive, and I'll get almost as much use out of it after you've gone as you will."

"Only if you *promise* to use it after I leave," Luna said, peering at me earnestly. Then her expression changed as her eyes opened wide and her forehead wrinkled in delight. "Maybe we can have some fun designing and making patterns *together*!"

"I'd really enjoy that, Luna. We still have a few days left in the winter holiday. Would you like to go to the fabric store tomorrow and look around for ideas?"

"That would be awesome!" Luna said, bouncing up and down excitedly on her car seat. "Oh my God–you're the *best*, Jade!"

The following day, we set out to the local fabric store to begin searching for material. We both agreed that we'd like to surprise each other with our initial designs, so we paid for our samples separately then we went home and began sketching some ideas. After supplying each other with our measurements, we set out crafting our garments. With Luna's measurements of 35-23-34, I wanted to make something sexy and flattering for her figure. While *she* worked in the evenings and on weekends on her design, I worked during the day while she was at school.

When the day finally came to reveal our designs to each other, we met in the living room like two kids at Christmas. We did rock-paper-scissors to see who would go first, and Luna won the first round.

"Okay," she said excitedly to me. "I've got your item wrapped up in this garment bag, so I want you to turn around before I reveal it."

"Now you've got *me* all excited," I said, turning around to face the windows looking out into the backyard. "Tell me when it's okay to turn around."

I heard Luna unzip her garment bag, followed by a slight rustling sound, then she giggled softly.

"Okay, I'm ready," she said.

I turned around and peered at a cream-colored linen mid-length dress with cropped sleeves and a small slit on each side of the lower hem.

"Wow," I said, widening my eyes. "It looks *gorgeous*! Can I try it on?"

"Absolutely," Luna smiled with a huge grin.

"Do you mind if I undress here?"

"It's just us girls," she nodded with a smile. "No one else is looking."

I kicked off my loafers then pulled my pants down and unzipped my blouse, laying them over the back edge of the sofa. Then I unzipped the back closure and stepped into the dress wearing only a bra and panties. The dress fit snuggly over my hips and ass, and the V-neck top hugged my bosom perfectly, creating a slim, tapered look.

"Can you zip me up in the back?" I said, turning around.

For the first time, I felt Luna's hands caress my bare skin as she closed the panels and zipped them together. I turned around to face her, feeling my nipples getting hard and my panties moistening.

"It fits perfectly," I gushed, swiping my hands down the side of the dress, stepping forward to see how much room I had to maneuver. "And the little side slits leave just enough room to move around comfortably. You absolutely *nailed* this one, Luna. How did you know linen was one of my favorite fabrics?"

Luna looked at me sheepishly and shrugged.

"I confess that I peeked in your closet when you weren't looking to get some ideas. I hope you like it."

"I love it!" I said. "It's classic, sexy, and timeless. Though I might not be able to wear it until summer. Because of that silly no-white-before-Memorial-Day rule."

"At least I'll see it on you before I leave," Luna smiled. "I was hoping you might also wear it when you come to visit me in France this summer."

"I'd love that Luna," I smiled, leaning in to kiss her on the cheek.

"Why don't you go for a walk down the hall to see how comfortably it moves with you?"

"Okay," I said, strutting down the hall using my best supermodel catwalk imitation, swinging my hips from side to side in an exaggerated manner as I stepped one foot in front of the other.

"Wow," Luna said. "It almost looks better from *behind* than from the front, if you don't mind my saying. Is there enough room for you to walk comfortably?"

"Absolutely," I said, swinging around and affecting a pouty model face as I strode back down the hall toward her. "There's just enough play in the skirt with the side slits to allow me to walk with a normal gait. This is the absolute perfect dress! Thank you, Luna, for making me such a pretty garment. You really do have a knack for this."

"The pleasure was all mine," Luna beamed. "But with a figure like yours, I suspect even a *potato sack* would look good on you."

"Hardly," I said. "But it's my turn now. Turn around while I get your surprise ready."

"Okay," Luna squeaked, barely able to contain herself as she turned to face the windows overlooking the backyard.

I pulled her two-piece garment out of a department store bag and held them up, one on top of the other.

"Okay," I said, excited to reveal my design. "You can turn around now."

When Luna flipped around and saw what I'd made, her eyes flew open and she jumped up and down excitedly.

"Oh my God—they're *beautiful!*" she exclaimed, moving in closer to examine the lacy camisole and matching silk shorts.

"I hope you don't think I was being too forward designing a sexy loungewear set for you," I said. "But I thought these would look beautiful on you and now that you're almost finished high school, I thought you might like something to make you feel all grown up."

"Are you *kidding* me?" she said. "I've always dreamed of owning something like this, but my parents would never let me wear them."

She stepped forward and pinched the fabric between her fingers, rubbing it softly.

"Is this...?"

"Yes," I smiled. "It's real silk. None of that fake polyester Victoria's Secret stuff for my pretty European model. I wanted to make a first-class outfit for a first-class girl."

"Can I try them on?" she said.

"Of course. That is, if you feel comfortable taking your clothes off—"

Luna practically ripped off her jeans and t-shirt then unclasped her bra and pulled down her panties, throwing them in a pile next to mine on the sofa. Seeing her for the first time naked, I couldn't help but glance down at her exquisite figure. Her breasts sat high and proud on her chest, pointing straight out like a Madonna corset, with large brown areolas and pink nubs. Her mound was shaved perfectly bald, and my mind suddenly wandered back to the memory of listening to her shaving in the bathtub while my pussy fluttered under my linen dress.

She pulled on the silky shorts first, then she lifted her arms as I watched the camisole slide down over her shoulders and her protruding tits. I was worried about getting the fit right over her uniquely shaped breasts, but when the straps fell over her shoulders, the fabric draped sexily over her mounds with just the right amount of cling and loose folds. And the lacy top hem swept down just enough to tastefully show off her tight cleavage without making it look trampy.

"How do I look?" Luna said, smiling at me sexily.

"*Mouth-watering*," I said, feeling my panties growing damper by the moment. "You could give any one of those Victoria Secret models a run for their money. How's the fit?"

"It clings to my body with just the right amount of drape. And the silk feels absolutely heavenly against my bare skin. Do you mind if I see what it looks like in your upstairs dressing mirror?"

"Of course," I said, taking her hand and leading her toward the stairs. "I was thinking the same thing."

When we got to my bedroom, Luna stepped in front of the full-length mirror and gasped. The soft baby-blue with cream-colored lace accents made her look sexy and innocent at the same time. While she peered at the front profile of her lingerie set, I ran my eyes over her tight ass perfectly framed by the clingy silk fabric.

"It fits me perfectly!" she gushed, twisting her body from side to side while she peered at herself in front of the mirror. "How does it look from behind?"

"Just as sexy as from the *front*," I smiled. "See for yourself."

Luna turned her body around then twisted her head to look at her reflection in the mirror.

"How did you get it to fit me so perfectly?" she said, pushing her butt out in a vampy pose. "It fits every curve of my body like a glove!"

"I've had a fair amount of time to study your body in my wet swimsuit in the hot tub these past few weeks. Your figure is indelibly imprinted on my brain."

"Thank you, Jade," Luna said, rushing up toward me and flinging her arms around my neck while she pressed her tits and hips against me.

As I hugged her softly, I desperately wanted to place my hand under her chin and kiss her, pulling her onto the bed only a few inches away. But somehow I managed to keep it together and release her after a few moments, while we continued admiring our fashion designs in the mirror.

If this was the best way to get her body pressing up against mine, I thought, I was already thinking of the *next* clothing design I had in mind for her.

5

Over the next few weeks, Luna and I continued to make increasingly sexy outfits for one another. My next design was a cut-out one-piece swimsuit with a large oval opening on both sides of her midsection that accentuated her curvy figure. For her part, she designed a matching lace bra and panty ensemble that took my lingerie set one step further. Feeling excited about carrying our mutual clothing design venture to the next level, I left a message for her on the fridge one afternoon while I went to the fabric store to shop for more material.

Luna,

Running some errands this afternoon. Should be home around 5:00 p.m. Feel like pizza tonight?

Jade

I received a text back from her when she got home from school saying pizza sounded great, but by then I'd finished most of my shopping so I headed back a bit earlier than planned. When I pulled into the driveway, I didn't open the garage door like usual because I wanted to sneak my new fabric design in without her seeing it.

Opening the door softly, I tiptoed down the hall and up the stairs, hoping to hide the material in my closet.

But as I approached my bedroom, I heard a soft buzzing sound and I paused at the partially closed door, peering through the crack. Luna was lying buck naked on my bed with a vibrator humming loudly between her legs. I recognized it immediately as my Rabbit vibrator and she was holding the end of it with two hands while she pressed the flapping ears tightly against her pussy.

Instantly aroused in a fit of passion, I placed the fabric bag down on the floor and unzipped my pants, thrusting my fingers under my soaking panties. As I watched Luna ramming the dildo in and out of her bare cunny, I trilled my clit rapidly, feeling my knees beginning to weaken. She looked even *more* beautiful with a soft flush filling her face and her pointy tits jiggling on her chest as she rolled her hips and flexed her arms, fucking herself with the buzzing vibrator.

As she began to arch her back and widen her mouth in mounting ecstasy, it took every ounce of my willpower not to barge through the door and take her into my arms. The more she tensed her body and arched her back, the closer my own orgasm steamrolled toward me. When she suddenly grunted and began jerking her body forward and back in the midst of a powerful orgasm, I felt my juices spraying all over my hand and jeans resting halfway down my thighs.

I was tempted to sneak away before she caught me lurking outside the door, but there was something about seeing the girl I'd fantasized about for the past two months naked on my bed that kept me hesitating in the hall. After she recovered from her orgasm, she pulled the still-buzzing Rabbit vibrator out of her pussy. Seeing her juices glistening on the whirring contraption made my pussy throb as two more steams of lubrication trickled down the inside of my thighs. When she reached over and pulled open my nightstand drawer to search for another toy, I smiled.

That's it, baby, I purred. *Go ahead and try out my entire collection. Give your momma a nice show.*

When she lifted the oversize Magic Wand vibrator out of the drawer, my heart fluttered.

You better be careful with that one, sweetie. It packs a hellova punch.

This was one of the few vibrators I owned that had a power cord, and Luna lifted herself off the bed, searching for the nearest outlet. While I watched her bend over, revealing the glistening slit between her legs as she plugged the device into the wall, I kicked off my jeans and panties, eager to free up my pussy for less restricted access. Something told me this show might go on for a while, and I planned on enjoying it to the fullest. But when she climbed back on the bed instead of lying back down face up, she surprised me by getting on all fours with her bare ass pointed directly in my direction.

Fuck me, I thought to myself. *You're making this damn near impossible for me, girl.* Now it was going to be even more difficult to restrain myself from barging through the door and pouncing on top of her.

As I watched her spread her knees apart then rest her chest on the bed as she angled her hips up in the air, I stood mesmerized outside the door. I could see her entire gleaming vulva from her bald pubis down over her splayed lips, all the way to her tight brown pucker. Even her swollen clit was visible from my position, poised like a ripe cherry at the junction of her folds under the bottom of her mound.

Oh, how I longed to be lying between her legs, taking her plump fruit into my mouth.

But when she flicked on the big vibrator and positioned the pulsating ball over her erect gland, I lost all sense of space and time. As her hips began to undulate against the vibrating head, I thrust three fingers inside my pussy and began fucking myself hard. I could see her tits hanging between the A-frame of her splayed legs, and when she grabbed one breast with her other hand and began squeezing it while she moaned in pleasure, I unbuttoned my own blouse and thrust my bra up under my neck, pinching my nipples.

I hadn't witnessed such an erotic sight in a very long time, and I bit my lip trying to remain silent while I watched the sexy nymph pleasuring herself. As I watched her juices pouring out of her snatch and rolling down the insides of her thighs, I could hear her cries and whimpers growing in urgency. But when she reached around behind her ass with her free hand and thrust two fingers into her pussy while she rocked back and forth on the bed, I almost lost it. I had to stop fingering myself for fear of falling off the cliff and making a commotion.

Besides, I wanted to save myself for the big finish. I wanted to dream that I was right there *with* her, grinding my sopping pussy against her while we came together.

As Luna began pumping her fingers harder into her hole, she turned her head sideways on the bed, and I saw the look of ecstasy on her face. As she opened her mouth wider approaching another orgasm, I suddenly felt my cunt clamping down on my fingers as I jetted my juices all over my palm. Seconds later, Luna emitted a loud squeal as she pulled her fingers out of her cunny and I saw her rosebud contracting in powerful convulsions while she pressed the vibrating ball of the magic wand hard against the base of her mound.

Oh my God, I panted outside my door, trying to control my breathing so as not to be heard.

Thinking that would be the end of it, I was surprised a few minutes later when Luna peered inside the drawer one more time then pulled out my favorite sex toy, the Osé vibrator. Designed to mimic the movement of a person's natural anatomy, the uniquely shaped device had a long bulbous finger-shaped projection that curled forward in rhythmic pulses to stimulate the front side of a woman's G-spot. The other part of the device had a small opening in the base with a flexible tongue designed to imitate the action of a person's mouth. When it was fully inserted into the vagina, the two parts together delivered an unforgettable experience unlike anything else, designed to give its recipient a blended, full-body orgasm.

Luna peered at the device with pinched eyebrows for a moment, turning it over in her hands trying to figure out how the various parts worked. Eventually, she found the power button on the base of the unit, and when she held it down I saw a small green LED light illuminate.

That's my girl, I smiled. *It takes a little getting used to, but if you just play with the buttons enough, you'll figure it out.*

Flipping the device upside-down, she noticed the control buttons under the base. She pressed one of the buttons, then her eyes lit up as the finger-shaped appendage began flexing toward her in a come-hither motion. When she pressed the little plus symbol next to the button, the finger began moving more rapidly. Shaking her head in shock, she ramped down the speed of the finger then tapped the other button. Suddenly, the aperture at the base of the unit began to pucker open and shut, mimicking the motion of a moving mouth. Luna leaned her head closer to the device, mesmerized by the strange object.

Pretty incredible, right? I muttered, teleporting my thoughts to her through the thin crack in the door. *You have no idea how heavenly it feels until you actually put it inside you.*

She turned all the power functions off, then sat up against my headboard with her knees hiked up toward her chest. Then she slowly inserted the long finger into her slit until the base was pressed firmly against her vulva. When she tapped the finger-control button on the base of the unit and felt it moving inside her, she groaned softly.

"Yes, Jade," she purred. "Finger my pussy while I look at your beautiful body."

I stepped away from the door, wondering if she'd seen my shadow moving in the hall. But when I peered back at her, her eyes were closed as she continued talking to herself. When she tapped the clitoral-control button, she slid her hips down while spreading her knees further apart.

"Oh God, Jade," she moaned. "That feels incredible. Lick my clit with your soft tongue. I want to feel your face against my pussy when I come."

Holy shit, I thought, plunging my fingers back into my dripping hole. *She's fantasizing about the device being my own fingers and mouth touching her instead of the artificial toy!*

Knowing she wanted me as much as I'd fantasized about having her, ratcheted up my pleasure tenfold as my juices began flowing out of my pussy in rivers. I was tempted to swing open the door and tell her I was waiting right here for her, but I didn't want to invade her privacy and embarrass her using my toys. I'd have to wait for another time to make my first move. But right now, I was going to *enjoy* this fantasy show to the fullest.

As she began to undulate her hips against the throbbing device, Luna tapped the plus button on the base of the unit, increasing the speed and intensity of the two simultaneous functions. Holding the base of the unit tightly against her snatch, she grabbed one of her tits with her other hand and moaned loudly.

"Fuck yes," she grunted. "Suck my clit while you finger my cunt, Jade. You feel so good, I'm going to come soon all over your face..."

Yes please, I hissed, watching her fuck herself with the animatronic device. My juices were now dripping all over my hand and my pants lying on the floor below my legs, and I wondered how I was going to put them back on and sneak past her without her knowing what I'd been doing.

"Jade!" she suddenly squealed. "I'm going to come. I'm going to come so hard all over your pretty face. Make me–*unghhh!*"

When I saw Luna climaxing again with the sexy toy embedded in her pussy, I watched her face contorted in sweet agony, wishing it was my face planted between her knees instead of the artificial vibrator. As her body quivered and writhed on the bed in the midst of another powerful climax, I clenched my jaw trying to control my breathing, pursing my lips to make sure she couldn't hear my own suppressed squeaks. It was most powerful orgasm I'd experienced in months, and it took almost a full minute for my contractions to stop pulsing inside me.

When I finally stopped shaking outside the door, Luna suddenly turned her wrist to look at her watch, then she got up off the bed and dashed into the washroom to clean off the vibrators. I looked at my phone, and realizing it was approaching five o'clock, I pulled up my pants and crept back downstairs. Then I quietly opened the front door and waited outside on the doorstep for a few minutes to allow Luna to put herself back together.

After three or four minutes, I opened the door with a flourish and called Luna's name to announce myself.

"Hello beautiful," I shouted. "I'm home. Are you hungry?"

I smiled listening to her scampering upstairs as she ran from my bedroom into her own. It looked like the two of us were going to continue our little cat-and-mouse game for a little longer. Holding the fabric store shopping bag in front of my crotch as I ascended the stairs to conceal the giant wet stain on the front of my jeans, I scurried into my room and changed into fresh clothes. After I stowed the shopping bag in my closet and washed the smell of my juices off my hands, I went downstairs and saw Luna sitting on the sofa watching TV like nothing had happened.

"How was your day today?" I asked, pressing my lips together to conceal my knowing smile.

"Pretty uneventful," Luna replied. "You?"

"I picked up some more material at the fabric store. I can't wait for you to see what I've got planned for my next surprise."

"I like surprises," Luna said, peering back at me from the sofa.

"Me too," I smiled. "Are you hungry?"

"Voracious," she said. "I could eat a horse."

That's not the only thing I could eat right now, I thought, gazing back at her like a Cheshire Cat.

6

____

For the next week or so, the sexual tension in the house continued to ramp up as Luna took more frequent baths, making little effort to conceal her increasingly noisy self-pleasuring activity. One day, not long after school ended, I came home from a shopping trip and saw her lying in the hot tub with a more flushed face than usual. As I began putting the groceries away in the cupboards, I glanced at her in the reflection of the microwave glass panel and noticed that she was positioned in the special spot where she could receive direct underwater stimulation to her private areas.

I turned around and motioned to her that I was coming out to join her, and she waved for me to come in. But this time, I didn't even bother going through the pretense of changing into a bathing suit as I stripped off my clothes and scampered out the back door, lowering my naked body into the swirling water.

"I hope you don't mind if I enjoy the hot tub in the *nude* this time," I said. "I think we've seen each naked enough times by now that there shouldn't be any more surprises."

"Of course not," she smiled. "I was thinking the same thing.

Though I have to admit I've been enjoying wearing this sexy new swimsuit you made for me."

"Are you finding the openings in the fabric provide enough stimulation from the underwater jets?"

"Yes," she said, subtly adjusting her position on the seat. "Although sometimes I wish there were a few *other* strategically placed holes for me to fully appreciate this experience."

"I know what you mean," I smiled. "I see you've found the special spot in the tub where you can receive an even *more* invigorating massage."

"It's pretty hard to miss," Luna nodded, spreading her legs wider apart under the churning water. "Is there a similar spot on the other side of the tub where you can enjoy it too?"

"As a matter of fact, there *is*," I grinned, positioning my pussy directly in front of the underwater jet shooting up from the base of the tub. "*Mmm*–that feels better."

"You seem to have quite a few toys in the household for stimulating your body," she smiled.

"How do you mean?" I asked coyly. "Like *what* other toys?"

"Um..." Luna hesitated as a deep flush rolled over her face.

"It's okay," I said. "I know that you found my secret stash of sex toys. I saw you using them one day when I came home a bit early."

"You don't mind?"

"Are you kidding me?" I said. "I enjoyed watching you almost as you did *using* them."

"Well now that we're not sharing secrets anymore," Luna smiled. "I heard you out in the hall that day. I enjoyed giving you a little show, hoping you might come in and join me on the bed."

"Oh, Luna," I gushed, feeling the powerful jet spraying against my tingling clit. "I've wanted you from the minute I first saw you–"

"The feeling was mutual," Luna said, looking me squarely in my eyes as her own pleasure beginning to escalate from the jet caressing her covered vulva.

She pulled her hands out of the water and stripped off her swimsuit, throwing it on the deck of the hot tub.

"Fuck it," she said. "No more playing around. I'm going to enjoy this hot tub the way it was intended. I want to come this time watching you orgasm with me."

"Yes, baby," I panted. "Come with me while I watch you. I'm already close."

"I'm coming, Jade," Luna suddenly grunted as her eyes glazed over.

"Uhnnn," I groaned, gazing at her as we both shuddered under the swirling water.

We watched our heads bobbing in spastic union for a few moments, then we both smiled.

"That took a lot longer to happen than I planned," I said.

"Why don't we go upstairs and *finish* this properly?" Luna smiled. "It's about time I felt your soft skin against me instead of these artificial jets or a silicone sex toy."

"Are you sure you want to do this?" I said, hardly believing my own ears. "I mean, we'd be overstepping the bounds of our arrangement..."

"We're both adults," Luna said. "What Ms. Laurent and my parents don't know won't hurt them. I need you so bad. Please make love to me, Jade."

"You're twisting my arm," I said. "But just to be sure the neighbors don't get suspicious, why don't you put your swimsuit back on before you get out of the tub? I'll join you in a few minutes after I make sure the coast is clear."

"Good idea," Luna said, pulling the suit off the deck and squeezing her body back into it under the cover of the water. "I'll be waiting for you in your bed upstairs."

The next two minutes seemed like an eternity as I thought about my sexy angel waiting for me naked and dripping wet. After a short waiting period, I glanced around me at the surrounding yards to make sure nobody was watching, then I scampered out of the hot tub and ran upstairs, not even bothering to dry off. When I saw Luna spread out naked on my bed with the covers pulled down, I jumped on the mattress next to her, wrapping my arms and legs tightly around her.

"Luna," I panted, feeling electrified from the sensation of her warm body next to mine. "I can't believe we're finally going to do this. I've waited so long..."

"Me too," Luna purred, pressing her hips and breasts against mine. "I always wondered what it would be like to make love to a woman. And I can't imagine a more perfect partner. I've grown very close to you these past few months."

"Oh baby," I sighed. "I feel exactly the same way. I haven't felt like this in such a long time."

"Is this your first time with a woman also?" she asked.

"No," I smiled. "But it's the first time with another woman I've felt so close to."

"Make love to me, Jade," she purred. "I want to feel your love as you caress me."

"Yes, baby," I said. "I'm going to love every square inch of your body."

I inserted my thigh between her legs and pulled it up toward her crotch, feeling her slippery lubrication coating the inside of her thighs. When I pressed my leg against her pussy, she moaned, thrusting her tongue into my mouth while we kissed each other passionately.

"Mmm," she hummed. "You feel so soft. I want to feel you *everywhere*."

"Oh you *will* baby," I said, edging myself lower down her body.

When I reached her neck, I nibbled on her skin then sucked her flesh into my mouth.

"I thought we were supposed to be careful about letting people know what we've been up to?" she said. "You're going to leave hickeys all over me!"

"Who's to say they were from *me*?" I smiled. "You're a big girl now. Isn't this what teenagers do to each other behind the portables at school?"

"You're very bad, Jade," Luna panted.

"You have *no* idea," I said.

Feeling her tits caressing the sides of my neck, I moved my face lower, swirling my tongue over her beautiful brown medallions while I sucked her erect nipples into my mouth with a loud popping sound. I'd dreamed of sucking her tits ever since I saw her in her tight sweater. Feeling her finally in my soft, pliant mouth was driving me insane with desire, and I could feel my juices coating her thighs as I rubbed my body against her. I lifted my face and squeezed her tits with my hands, kneading the firm flesh between my fingers.

"You have no idea how much I've wanted to touch you like this," I said, blowing softly on her puckering teats.

"Oh, I have an idea," she groaned. "Between the sexy lingerie set you designed for me and the cutaway swimsuit, you seemed to be overly focused on my girl parts."

"You got that right," I said. "Do you mind if I take a moment to fulfill one particular fantasy I've been harboring ever since I saw these beautiful breasts up close and personal?"

"I can't imagine what you're thinking," Luna smiled. "But I want you to do everything a woman can do to another woman in the remaining time we have together. I don't ever want to forget this time we have left."

I lifted my body up and knelt over her torso with my knees straddling her chest, then I lowered my dripping pussy onto one of her tits. When she felt my warm vulva touching her skin, she reached down and grabbed her breast with two hands, rolling it back and forth over my throbbing slit.

"Oh *God*, Luna," I panted, feeling her erect nipple pressing into my opening. "Fuck me with your beautiful breasts. That feels incredible."

"This is way better than playing with a *sex toy*," she said, smiling up at me.

"Even that special *white* one with the bendy finger and realistic tongue action?"

"There's no comparison," she said. "You're softer, warmer, and wetter. And besides, you can't make *love* to a sex toy, even one that imitates human movement so well."

"Oh, Luna," I said, bending forward to kiss her. "I've fallen in love with you these past few months. I don't ever want you to leave."

"Let's enjoy the little time we have together to the fullest," she smiled. "We have a lot of catching up to do."

"Mmm," I said, rolling my sopping pussy all over her firm mounds. "You feel so good, baby. Keep tribbing me with your tits."

As Luna flapped her breast against my quivering pussy, I moaned louder and louder into her mouth, rapidly approaching my peak. Sensing I was getting close, Luna grabbed the sides of my hips, slowing my movement.

"Can I feel you come in my *mouth* instead this first time?" she asked. "I want to watch your face while I kiss you in your most intimate place. This has been *my* fantasy these past few months."

"As long as you let me return the favor," I said, lifting my head and gazing into her eyes. "Are you sure you're going to know how to do this?"

"How hard can it be?" she smiled. "I'll just imitate the action of the Osé sex toy that I used while you were watching me a few days ago."

"Mmm," I nodded. "I've come many times imagining that was another woman's mouth on my pussy. But something tells me this time it's going to be a hundred times better."

"Only a *hundred*?" Luna smirked.

"Come here," I said, shimmying my hips overtop of her head and lowering my steaming cunt onto her rosebud lips. "Suck my pussy with those pretty lips."

"Mmmm," Luna moaned, feeling my erect nub in her mouth as I coated her face with the juices streaming out of my slit.

She looked up at me and grabbed both of my tits with her two hands, squeezing them firmly. Seeing her pretty face framed by my thighs straddling her head drove me crazy, and when we locked eyes expressing how close we felt to one another at that moment, a tear rolled down my cheek.

"Luna," I groaned. "I love you, baby. It won't take me long now. Can I come on your sweet, beautiful face?"

"*Mm-hmm,*" Luna nodded excitedly, squeezing my tits with three quick pulses to show that she returned the sentiment.

"Here's it comes, baby," I gushed. "Oh God, I'm *cumming. Nnngh!*"

As my orgasm washed over me, my entire body began shaking as I gushed all over Luna's flushed cheeks. She blinked her eyes in surprise but never stopped caressing my clit as she sucked it tightly in her mouth. While I sat convulsing over her face, she peered up at me with her aquamarine eyes, cupping my breasts lovingly in her hands. When I finally finished coming, I lifted myself off her and lay down next to her, tasting my juices on her lips as I intertwined my tongue with hers.

"That was *incredible,*" I said, pulling back to look into her eyes.

"Was I okay for my first time?"

"*Okay*?" I said, widening my eyes. "You're a natural at this. Now I'm going to miss you all the more when you leave. Nothing's going to make up for you being gone."

"Not even that special rabbit vibrator with the rotating shaft and the flapping ears?"

"Not even *that,*" I laughed, leaning in to kiss her again. "But it's your turn now. I've been dreaming about touching *another* part of your body for quite a while. It's time for me to taste *you* and feel you come in my mouth now."

"I'd like that," Luna smiled. "But we've still got a few days to explore each other's bodies. Can you *hold* me when you make love to me this time? I want to feel *every* part of you rubbing up against me when we come together."

"*God* yes," I said. "You've been reading my mind."

I rolled Luna onto her back then lifted myself on top of her, straightening my legs between hers as I pressed my pubis against her mound. She lifted her knees and spread her legs apart as she angled her hips upward, pressing her wet vulva against mine. We both moaned and grabbed each other's heads, pulling our lips together. As our tongues danced in each other's mouths, we began to rock our hips in unison. I could feel Luna's tits pressing against mine, and my entire body tingled from the sensation of her rubbing up against me.

She rocked her hips awkwardly against mine, trying to lock our pussies together, but in our missionary position it was difficult to get traction on both of our clits. I lifted my body and moved up a few inches, straddling her stomach with my thighs, then I pressed my sex down over her bald mound. She spread her legs further apart at the same time, tilting her hips upward until our glands touched. When she felt my hard clit rubbing against hers, she groaned deeply into my mouth, pressing her fingers into my back.

As we began to hump each other, I could hear the sound of our wet pussies smacking together while our juices rolled down the insides of both our thighs. Feeling her warm flesh pressed against mine was everything I'd dreamed of, and it didn't take long for me to feel the familiar pangs of a powerful orgasm rising within me again.

"Luna," I panted. "I've wanted to feel you like this for so long. I'm going to come soon. Let me feel you come *with* me while I hold you in my arms."

"Yes, Jade," Luna grunted. "I feel so close to you. Oh *God*!"

Suddenly she dug her nails hard into my back as she squeezed my hips tightly with her thighs, grunting loudly into my mouth. Feeling her hot pussy against mine when she came soon pushed me also over the edge also, as I sprayed my juices all over her gaping hole while I pressed my cunt hard against her. As we both squealed and groaned into each other's mouths, I held her tightly until we finished coming. When we finally finished quivering in each other's arms, I lay down beside her, softly stroking her cheek as I gazed into her eyes.

"Do you know what we French girls call an orgasm?" she said, smiling at me.

"I have no idea," I said, shaking my head.

"We call it *la petite mort*," she said. "It means little death."

"That's funny," I chuckled. "I guess that's kind of fitting, given all the convulsions we experience at the moment of climax and the way we go limp afterwards. But that reminds me. I haven't spent nearly as much time as I'd hoped learning your language while you've been with me. There's so much more I was hoping you could teach me."

"I'll be happy to," Luna said, suddenly rolling back on top of me. "But something tells me you've still got plenty to teach me too."

As our bodies melded back together again, I couldn't help smiling. This cultural exchange program had been far more beneficial for both of us than I'd ever imagined.

VOLUME FIVE

THE ORIENT EXPRESS

1

Entering the Gare du Nord terminal in Paris, I peered up at the soaring glass ceiling enclosing the cavernous central hall. Knowing it was the busiest train station in Europe, I held my arms close to my sides to protect my valuables from ever-present pickpockets. Designed by the famous French architect Jacques Hittorff in the Beaux-Arts style of the mid-nineteenth century, I marveled at the ornate cast-iron pillars supporting the enormous structure. It was a clear sunny day, and bright beams of light angled through the windows, illuminating the shiny trains resting beside their platforms. I glanced at my ticket and headed toward gate eighteen, where I was about to embark on a five-day/four-night tour of Europe aboard the most famous train in history.

Passing through the pastoral countryside of southern France and the deep valleys of the Swiss Alps, the Orient Express wound its way through seven countries, terminating at the gateway to Asia in Istanbul. With its storied past and recently refurbished equipment, I was looking forward to being pampered in the five-star dining car and my own private cabin on the traveling caravan. I'd heard so much about the glamor and prestige of the famous line, and as I approached the black-and-gold vintage train cars sitting by the platform, my heart began to flutter in excitement.

Near the front of the train, a porter wearing a brass-buttoned uniform and white gloves checked my ticket then helped me up the steps into the forward compartment. When I stepped into the carriage, I was shocked at how opulent it looked. The main salon was decorated with sumptuous velour upholstery, polished cherry wood paneling, crystal lanterns, and giant windows framed with royal blue curtains. More beautiful than any luxury hotel I'd ever stayed in, the setting literally took my breath away.

"Oh my God," I muttered to the porter. "It's like I've entered a whole different world. This isn't like any train I've been on before."

"That's a common reaction from our first-time travelers," he said. "Our owners have spared no expense in recreating the feel and authenticity of the original train. If you like the main seating area, I think you'll be very pleased with your cabin. I see you've chosen the grand suite."

"Yes," I nodded. "I figured if I'm going to splurge on a luxury train ride, I might as well go all the way."

"I think you'll find the extra space is quite comfortable. You've got three large viewing windows, your own sitting area, and a large private washroom."

"Well if it's anything like the rest of the train," I said, tracing my fingers along the luxurious upholstery as we passed by the four-person seating booths, "I'm sure I'll be delighted."

We walked through two more carriages down a narrow passageway then he stopped by a polished wooden door with a brass handle.

"Here we are, madam," he said, opening the door and motioning for me to enter ahead of him with his gloved hand.

I stepped into the anteroom and gasped out loud. The entire chamber gleamed in a mixture of knurled walnut paneling, crystal light fixtures, and suede seat coverings. The king-size bed was festooned with plush Egyptian-cotton linens and blue-and-gold embroidered cushions, with outside light streaming in the huge viewing windows lining the entire side of the compartment."

"It's...*breathtaking*," I said, hardly believing my eyes. "It's the most beautifully bedroom I've ever seen. Is this all just for *me*?"

"Yes, ma'am," the porter said, opening another door next to the sitting area. "As is this private ensuite bathroom."

I peered inside the washroom, my eyes opening as wide as saucers.

Almost every surface was covered in polished alabaster marble. From the large, glass-enclosed walk-in shower to the brass taps on the vanity to the separately enclosed toilet, everything reeked of first class. It even had a separate, sit-down makeup table, replete with Lalique crystal lamps.

"If I ever get to heaven," I sighed. "This is what I hope it looks like."

"I'm glad you like it, ma'am," the porter said. "As part of your grand suite package, you also have twenty-four-hour butler service, private in-cabin dining, and free-flowing champagne for the duration of your trip."

"Okay, so *wait*," I chuckled. "Are you sure I'm not *already* in heaven?"

The porter set my bags down on the floor and backed up toward the entrance door.

"Please, make yourself comfortable," he said. "If you need anything at all, press this button and your butler will call upon you shortly. Dinner in the main cabin will be served starting at seven p.m. But the bar is open twenty-four-seven. I hope you enjoy your stay with us."

"I only wish it could be longer," I smiled, discreetly handing him a ten-Euro tip. "Are you sure this train doesn't go any further than Istanbul?"

"For now, at least," he said. "That's the end of the line. But I've heard rumors our operator is considering extending the service into the Middle East and beyond, following the path of the Silk Road used by Marco Polo."

"Now that would be a truly memorable journey," I nodded. "It *is* called the Orient Express, after all."

———

After the porter left, I unpacked my bags and changed into something more befitting the glamorous setting, then I went into the washroom to touch up my makeup. When I finished, I looked at myself in the full-length dressing mirror and nodded in satisfaction. I'd chosen to wear a form-fitting, mid-length red silk dress with black leather Christian Louboutin heels that showcased my long, well-toned legs. As the train began to pull out of the station, I pulled the door to my cabin closed behind me and headed toward the bar car.

Let's see if the guests on this caravan are as interesting as the rest of the train, I smiled.

When I reached the bar car, I noticed a scattering of passengers chatting in the plush velour booths beside the window. I peered up toward the bar and saw an elegant woman sitting alone on one of the stools with her back toward me. She was wearing a cream-colored lace embroidered dress, and I glanced down to see her slender and shapely legs crossed under the brass railing. I walked up to the counter and smiled at the bartender.

"Good evening, madam," he said. "Would you like something to drink?"

"Yes, thank you," I said, looking at the row of liquor bottles lining the wall behind him. I was about to order a Grey Goose martini when I noticed the woman was cradling a tall tulip glass filled with a pale yellow mixture with bubbles rising to the surface. "I think I'll have what the lady's having."

"Dom Perignon it *is*," he nodded. He pulled a magnum off the shelf and carefully loosened the cork to let out the air before tilting the bottle over a carved crystal glass and sliding it toward me.

"May I join you?" I said, glancing at the lady sitting next to me.

"By all means," she smiled, uncrossing her legs and lifting her knee over her opposite leg.

As I sat down and turned my stool to face her, I noticed for the first time her plunging neckline and deep cleavage pressing her plump breasts together. She had long auburn-colored hair, styled with curly ringlets framing her pretty face. She looked to be around my age, but with slightly darker skin. She had a vaguely European look to her, and as she peered at me with her smoldering eyes, I felt my panties beginning to moisten.

"Cheers," I said, holding up my glass.

"Santé," she replied, clinking her champagne flute against mine.

"This is quite the experience, isn't it?" I said, looking around me at the ornately decorated cabin.

"Is this your first time?" she said with a French accent.

"Aboard the Orient Express? Yes. How about you?"

"This is my third trip. I find the experience to be quite stimulating."

"Are you referring to the amazing views?" I said, peering outside the window behind her at the passing Paris streetscape.

"That, and you meet the most interesting people on this voyage," she nodded. "We're all captive on this little train while we're traveling, and you get to know everybody pretty well."

"I can imagine," I said, flittering my eyes downward to take in her voluptuous figure. Her nipples were pressing hard against the sheer lacy fabric, and I crossed my legs, feeling my pussy growing wetter by the moment.

"Where are you from?" she said, peering down at my exposed thighs as she took another sip of her champagne. "You don't have a British, Aussie, or Kiwi accent, so I'm guessing you're either American or Canadian."

"I'm from Chicago," I said, chuckling at her deductive powers. "How about you?"

"I'm from the Alsace region of France, near the German border."

"I thought I recognized some Continental genes in your appearance. You're very pretty."

"As are you," she said, placing her hand on my knee and sliding it softly up my thigh. "You American girls always take such good care of your bodies. I like how you're so toned and fit. We Europeans take a much more laissez-faire approach to our fitness."

"Thank you," I said, feeling the soft hairs on the top of my thighs standing erect as her hand caressed my skin. Suddenly I wished I'd remembered to shave the full length of my legs more recently.

"I'm Jade, by the way," I said, extending my hand to distract attention from the other passengers glancing at us nearby.

"Adele," she said, clasping my hand and squeezing it gently. Even the touch of her hand against mine sent a chill through my spine.

"So, what do people do to pass their time for five straight days on this little chugger?" I asked, trying to regain my composure.

"Besides eating and drinking most of the time?" she chuckled. "Most people curl up with a book next to the window to watch the passing scenery. But at meal time, everybody gets together in the dining car, where we can mingle a bit more comfortably."

"Speaking of drinking," I said, realizing the bartender had already replenished my glass three times while I'd been talking. "I'm already starting to feel a bit tipsy. If I don't get off this bar stool soon, I'm afraid I'll fall over. I think curling up in one of those comfortable booths by the window is just what I need about now. Would you care to join me?"

"Perhaps a little later," she said, rising up from her stool. "Right now I need to make a trip to the ladies' room. But I look forward to meeting you again soon, lovely Jade."

While I watched her head down the hall toward the public lavatory, I couldn't help staring at her tight ass in her form-fitting dress as her buttocks flexed sexily under the sheer lacy fabric. I staggered to the nearest seat a few feet from the bar and rested my head against the backrest as I peered out over the passing landscape of the French countryside. I felt surprisingly lightheaded for only having had three drinks. Whether it was from drinking on an empty stomach or from the passing vineyards rushing by my window or from the excitement of meeting this mysterious and sexy woman, I couldn't be sure. Either way, my trip aboard the Orient Express had gotten off to an exciting start.

As I rubbed my thighs together thinking of the way she'd touched me, Adele suddenly passed by me and took a seat four booths down, sitting on the edge of the aisle, facing toward me. At first, I was disappointed that she hadn't decided to join me in my section, and I wondered if she just hadn't noticed me with my back turned away from her. But when she peered up at me and smiled, I nodded to acknowledge her reaction. I didn't want to intrude on her personal space, but what she did next left little doubt that she was far from being done with me. She lifted her left leg and placed her foot on top of the seat cushion next to her and hiked up her dress a few inches, revealing her bare, glistening pussy. Then she placed her hand between her thighs and began circling her fingers over the top of her slit.

I looked around me to see if anyone else could see what she was doing, but fortunately all the other guests were sitting snugly against their windows, either reading a book or quietly gazing outside. Because we were the only two people in the compartment sitting on the outside edges of our booths, we had a direct view of each other. At first, I sat dumbfounded watching her play with herself, shocked at her audacious display of carnality, but as my panties grew wetter and wetter watching her, I looked around me to make sure the coast was clear, then I lifted my ass off my seat and pulled my panties down over my ankles and placed them inside my purse. Then I pushed my hand under my dress and slid my fingers up my thighs until they reached my sopping sex.

When they touched my burning clit, I gasped from how turned on I was, and Adele smiled at me from the other end of the cabin. I didn't have the courage to hike up my dress the way she had for fear that a passing porter or passenger might catch me in the act, but it certainly didn't stop me from fingering myself furiously while I watched the sexy French woman touching herself. Adele spread her legs further apart, exposing her bald, glistening snatch, then she thrust two fingers deep into her hole as she began finger-fucking herself with her flexing arm muscles.

I could hear the rumbling of the train as it passed speedily over the tracks, and the imagery of our pleasing ourselves in this strange but exciting public place elevated my passion even higher. As I felt my pleasure beginning to radiate throughout my body, I couldn't help squirming in my seat and pinching my nipples with my free hand. Apparently, Adele was equally turned on by the erotic scene, with her mouth beginning to part from her own rising pleasure while she stared back at me from across the aisle.

I could tell that she was nearing the crest of her pleasure as her face began to flush and her hand began moving more vigorously in and out of her dripping pussy. I began to feel my own orgasm rapidly approaching, and I pressed my hand harder up against my burning clit, unaware that my own dress was now hiked up near the top of my thighs, exposing my own bald and glistening vulva. Suddenly, a deep flush rolled over both of our faces as we began jerking spastically in our seats with our bodies consumed in a powerful simultaneous orgasm. We didn't take our eyes off each other the whole time while we gazed at one another with our mouths wide agape.

It must have taken a full thirty seconds for my contractions to subside, and when my orgasm finally receded, I slumped in my seat with my legs still spread wide apart. It was only then that I noticed in horror that someone *else* had been watching us the whole time. Just a few feet behind Adele in the next compartment sat a young teenage girl peering through the crack in the seats with wide eyes, staring directly toward me. I closed my legs immediately and pulled my dress down over my thighs, then squiggled over closer to the window, shocked and humiliated. As I looked out the glass with my heart beating a million miles an hour, I felt my juices slowly trickling out of my wet pussy while I reflected on the exciting moment Adele and I had shared in the open compartment of the famed transcontinental express.

2

____

After I'd had a chance to calm down, I rested my head against my seat cushion and peered out over the passing landscape. The neatly spaced rows of vineyards provided a hypnotic counterpoint to the stimulating view of Adele playing with herself across the cabin, and before long I felt my eyelids grow heavy as I began to nod off. But just before I was about to pass out, I caught some movement from Adele's end of the carriage. The girl who'd been spying on us suddenly stood up and began sidestepping her way out of her cubicle.

She looked to be of middle eastern origin, with caramel-colored skin and large brown doe eyes. Her hair was pulled back into a pony-tail, and with her high cheekbones and puffy lips, I was immediately struck by how beautiful she was. She could have easily passed for a young fashion model, but when she stepped out into the aisle, I gasped. Wearing a mid-length plaid skirt and matching green blazer with bow tie, it was obvious that she was just a schoolgirl. I couldn't make out how old she was, but from the shape of her body barely concealed by the short skirt and her bulging white blouse under her blazer, she certainly looked all grown up to me.

When she caught me staring at her, she winked at me playfully, then turned away and began walking toward the opposite end of the compartment. She hesitated for a moment outside the door to the public lavatory, then hiked up one side of her skirt, revealing an exquisitely toned and completely bare ass. Before entering the restroom, she glanced back at me and tilted her head, beckoning for me to follow her.

What the fuck? I thought to myself, shaking my head at my incredible streak of luck. *Was everybody on this train oversexed and ready to jump on top of anyone they happened to bump into?*

I paused for a moment, contemplating my predicament. I didn't even know if the girl was of legal age to have sex. I took a closer look at her booth and saw a middle-aged man wearing a neatly pressed suit sitting close to the aisle. He had her same dark complexion and was reading a newspaper, seemingly oblivious to the sexually charged energy in the room. It seemed obvious to me that he was the girl's father or guardian, and I suspected he wouldn't look kindly upon my taking advantage of his daughter's youthful ardor.

But why was she dressed so provocatively, and why did she want me to join her in the lavatory? Had anyone *else* in the compartment noticed her libidinous display and was watching to see if I would join her? I glanced around the cabin and noticed that everyone was either staring outside their windows or had their heads bowed down tapping on their phones or laptop computers. If I was going to do something, I'd have to act soon before her father became suspicious of her extended absence.

Feeling the moisture beginning to accumulate once again between my thighs, I raised myself out of my seat and began walking in the direction of the lavatory. When I passed Adele's booth, she peered up at me and smiled. With her body facing away from the direction of the girl's booth immediately behind her, I had no idea if she was aware of the special connection I'd made with the other passenger. But from the look of her swelling nipples in her form-fitting dress, she still appeared to be charged up from our earlier encounter.

As I passed by the girl's cubicle, her father glanced up from his newspaper and we nodded politely toward each other. Not wanting him to catch onto my lascivious intent, when I reached the closed door of the lavatory, I ducked into the adjacent cubbyhole near the train's exit door and leaned against the side wall with my heart pounding in my chest.

Holy shit! I cursed under my breath. *Was I really contemplating going through with this? What if we were found out? What if someone else needed to use the washroom while we were both inside?* It would be impossible to extricate ourselves without the other person knowing what we were up to in there. What if her *father* needed to use the washroom while we were busy making love to each other inside?

For a moment, I contemplated returning to my seat and dispensing with the whole idea. But the streams of lubrication running down the inside of my thighs was giving me second thoughts. When would I ever have a chance like this again? It's not every day that you get propositioned by a comely young schoolgirl to have a secret tryst with her on board the most famous train in the world.

Fuck it, I hissed, stepping forward to the lavatory door and tapping on it gently. Seconds later, the door opened a few inches and the girl peered out at me. I hesitated, not knowing what to say, then she reached out and pulled me inside, locking the door behind us. I looked at her with wide eyes, wondering what I had gotten myself into.

"Are you sure you want to do this?" I mumbled. "What about your father? How old are–"

The girl suddenly pulled me toward her, thrusting her tongue into my mouth while she pressed her hips and breasts against mine. When I felt her warm body against me and her tongue sliding over my teeth, everything else melted away as my hands began roaming over her curvy body. She tried to hike up my dress over my hips and press her hand between my legs, but I knew we didn't much time for the usual foreplay. I placed my hands under her armpits and lifted her ass up onto the edge of the sink, pressing her torso against the mirror. Then I lifted her plaid skirt and buried my face in her moist pussy.

At this point I no longer cared if she was of legal age. I intended to give her the best head she'd ever had, if indeed she'd ever had oral sex of *any* kind before. She had a narrow patch of pubic hair on her otherwise hairless mound, and as I sucked her swollen clit into my mouth, she placed her heels on top of the vanity and pulled my head hard into her cunt as she began squirming and moaning in delight. I was tempted to lift my hand to her mouth to muffle her squeals, but I figured the clattering of the train's metal wheels on the tracks was sufficient to drown out our mutual sounds of ecstasy.

Instead, I reached up and began unbuttoning her blouse, threading my hand inside her placket and squeezing her firm tits. I was surprised how large they were for a girl her age, and as her gushing juices began to coat the front of my face while I ate her out, I hooked my thumbs under the bottom of her bra and forced it up over top of her bosom. When I felt her bare melons filling my hands, I moaned along with her in rising pleasure. My own clit was throbbing between my outspread legs in my squatted position, and I would have loved to have ground it against her tender pussy, but I knew it would be difficult in the tight confines of the train lavatory to find enough room to properly scissor our bodies together.

Besides, I was enjoying eating the young girl's pussy and listening to her squeals of pleasure as I ravished her dripping cunny like it was my last meal. As she squirmed wildly on the edge of the counter, she placed her hands over the back of my head and began to dig her nails into my scalp. It was becoming apparent to me that she was nearing the crest of her pleasure, and as her squeals turned to impassioned whimpering, I placed her teats between my thumbs and forefingers and pinched her nipples firmly as she dug her nails ever-harder into my flesh.

Just when I thought I wouldn't be able to stand the pain any longer, her body suddenly lurched and she humped forward, jerking spastically over my head while she uttered a deep guttural moan. I held her close as I felt her juices pouring out of her hole and down over the front of my chin until she stopped heaving overtop of me. When she finally stopped moving, I pulled my face away from her pussy and she pushed herself off the edge of the counter and turned toward the mirror to pull her bra back in place and button herself back up. Then she turned around and glanced at me, reaching for the lock on the door.

"Thank you," she said with a faint Arabic accent, then she opened the door a crack and peered outside to make sure the coast was clear.

"*Wait*," I said, grasping her hand. "Can I see you again?"

"I better return to my seat before my father gets suspicious. Maybe if you can find a way to pass me your room number..."

I smiled at the girl and squeezed her hand as she left the compartment, then I closed and latched the door behind her. I'd never felt such a thrill in all my life, and I had matters of my own that needed attending to. Whether it was the possibility of having had sex with an underage girl, or the fact that we'd done it only a few feet away from her waiting father or the sheer audacity of having sex with a stranger in the train's public lavatory, I still felt incredibly turned on. As I hiked my dress up over my knees and plunged my hand between my legs, trilling my clit furiously while I bent over the stainless steel sink, I began to plot how I might entice the girl into a more comfortable setting to properly make love to her.

3

———————

After cumming hard bent over the sink reliving my exciting liaison with the pretty schoolgirl, I returned to my seat in the main cabin and fell asleep with my head resting against the window. I awoke two hours later with a rumbling stomach, and noticing that the bar car had almost emptied out, I approached the bartender asking where I could get a bite to eat.

"Excuse me, sir," I said. "Which way is it to the dining car?"

"We have *two*, madam," he said. "The Cote D'Azur is the next car toward the front of the train, and the Hagia Sophia is the adjacent car to the rear."

"What's the difference?" I asked, wondering why in the world they would need two dining cars.

"The Cote D'Azur provides a continental menu, whereas the Hagia Sophia offers middle eastern fare."

"Wow, okay," I said, shaking my head at the continuing opulent array of choices on the luxury line.

I hesitated for a moment, then turned toward the aft section of the train, hoping to see another glimpse of the mysterious Arab girl. When I entered the adjoining carriage, my eyes widened at the sight that greeted me. The dining tables were immaculately set with neatly pressed white linen tablecloths, fine china, crystal drinking glasses, and sumptuous red velvet chairs. Most of the chairs were already occupied, but towards the rear of the compartment I noticed Adele sitting with the Arabian father and daughter pair, and I approached the table, motioning to the open seat.

"Do you have room for one more?" I asked, peering toward the gentleman.

"Of course," he said, rising politely and motioning for me to take the available seat.

I smiled toward the girl seated next to him at the window and nodded at Adele sitting next to me.

"I'm Jade," I said, extending my hand toward the gentleman.

"Omar," the man said. "And this is my daughter, Leila.

"And this lovely lady–" he said, motioning toward Adele.

"*Adele*–yes," I blushed. "We met earlier in the bar car."

"Perfect," he said, smiling toward his daughter. "I guess I'm the lucky one who'll be enjoying the company of three charming women over dinner this evening."

"Is this your first trip aboard the Orient Express?" I said, trying to break the awkward sexual tension at the table.

"Oh no," he said. "I make this trip often to visit my daughter in Paris. She's studying at the École Internationale."

"Oh?" I said, eager to hear more details about the mysterious girl. "What grade?"

"Lycée troisième," the girl said in a perfect French accent.

"My French is a little rusty," I smiled. "I'm not quite sure how that equates to our American education system."

"It's equivalent to grade 12 in the United States," Adele clarified.

"So you're a *senior* then," I nodded. "That would put you around seventeen–"

"I just turned eighteen," Leila replied matter-of-factly.

"You must be looking forward to graduating," I said, relieved to hear that she'd reached the age of majority. "I understand the Ecole Internationale is one of Europe's most exclusive private schools. Have you thought about where you'd like to go to college?"

"I've been accepted to Cambridge, La Sorbonne, and Harvard. But I'm leaning toward Harvard. I've never been to the United States–"

"I'd be happy to show you around if you'd like to visit. I have friends in the Boston area who I'm sure would be happy to put you up while you tour the campus."

"Really?" Leila said, her eyes perking up. "Where do you live in the States?"

"I'm from Chicago, but I do business in New England quite often. If you let me know when you'd like to come, I'm sure I could work my schedule around to accommodate you."

"That's very generous of you, Jade," Omar said, noticing the waiter approaching our table. "But we can talk about these matters later. Who's ready for something to eat?"

"I'm so hungry I could eat a horse, as we say in America," I said, winking at Leila.

"Well I don't know about *that*," Omar chuckled. "But I believe they serve lamb and Moroccan chicken if you prefer Arabian dishes."

"I'm definitely ready to sample more of your local fare," I smiled, feeling Leila tapping the outside of my foot under the table.

After we all ordered our meals, Adele excused herself to freshen up in the lavatory, and I took the opportunity to move over to the seat next to the window so I could be closer to Leila. When Adele returned, we talked about our travel plans and vocations. Omar ran an import-export business out of Istanbul and Adele was a finance executive with Commerzbank. The two of them struck up a conversation about foreign exchange rates, and before long Omar agreed to open an account at her bank. He then offered to let us stay at his villa on the Black Sea while we were in Turkey, to which both Adele and I readily agreed. Whether we were just happy to find any excuse to stay together during our layover or we were equally smitten by his beguiling daughter, was unclear. Either way, I was in no hurry to break up our happy little coterie.

When our meal service started with a shared plate of freshly baked pita and hummus, I noticed that Leila was growing increasingly frisky playing footsies with me under the table. By the time our main courses arrived, she'd already kicked off her shoes and was caressing the inside of my calves with her bare foot. Growing more emboldened by her father's seeming distraction with Adele's sexy lace dress and her continued efforts to solicit his banking business, she forced my knees apart and slowly began pressing her foot further up under my dress toward my bare crotch. When the ball of her foot began rubbing against my slippery vulva and twitching clit, I had a hard time concentrating on eating my meal. After a few minutes, Omar peered over at me, noticing my elevated breathing rate and soft moaning.

"Are you enjoying your lamb, Jade?" he said.

"Oh yes," I sighed, trying to keep my composure while his daughter foot-fucked me under the table. "It's quite...*succulent.*"

"Shakriya is one of our most popular dishes in Turkey," he nodded. "But the chefs here seem to have a special knack for bringing out its unique flavors. I'll have to ask them what their secret ingredient is."

"Yes," I moaned. "They seem quite skilled. I haven't enjoyed a meal quite this stimulating in a long time."

As he and Adele continued chatting about their growing banking partnership, I dared not even *look* at Leila for fear of betraying what she was doing to me under the table. Just when I thought it couldn't possibly get any more awkward and titillating, she suddenly thrust her big toe inside my pussy, curling the rest of her foot against my burning clit. I gasped in surprise, and Omar peered over at me in alarm.

"Are you alright, Jade?" he said. "Are you choking on something?"

"No," I said, bringing my napkin to my mouth to distract attention from my rapidly escalating arousal. "A piece of lamb just went down the wrong way. I'll have to slow down a bit while I'm eating. I think I'm just getting a little carried away with this sumptuous dish."

"It's definitely meant to be savored," he said, smiling at me politely. "But watch out for those spices. There's quite a bit of garlic and paprika in there. It'll burn your mouth if you're not careful."

"Yes," I panted. "I can feel it burning already."

"How about *you*, dear?" Omar said, turning to look at his unusually quiet daughter. "Are you enjoying your meal equally as much?"

"Yes father," Leila said. "I'm just enjoying listening in on your conversation with Adele. I find the world of finance fascinating."

"I'm glad you find it interesting," he said. "I'm looking forward to placing you in an important position in my business when you graduate from Harvard."

"Yes father," Leila nodded obediently while flexing her toes inside my dripping cunt.

As Omar and Adele continued their conversation, Leila quietly picked away at her dish with her knife and fork clinking against the fine china while she pretended to be absorbed in their discussion. Before long, the combination of her deft toe-fucking and tickling of my clit with the rest of her foot brought me to the brink of climax, and I fought valiantly to maintain my composure as my orgasm quickly swept over me. Trying to remain still in my chair, I couldn't help expressing the joy in my face as a deep rash suddenly poured over my cheeks and my eyes began to water from the intense pleasure emanating within my body.

Noticing my discomfort once again, Omar turned toward me with a concerned expression.

"Too much garlic?" he said, offering me a glass of water.

"Too much *something*," I said, gulping down the water trying to keep his attention focused above the table. "But it's very stimulating. I think I just need to acclimate more to your customs and cuisine. I'm looking forward to enjoying more of these delicacies once I land in your country."

"I'm looking forward to sharing more of our culture with *both* of you as my guests," he nodded, turning toward his daughter. "Don't you agree, Leila? We'll have to show these women some proper Turkish hospitality."

"Absolutely father," Leila said, beaming at both Adele and me. "There's so much more I'd love to show these lovely ladies."

For the rest of the meal, the four of us talked about our past experiences and future plans, while Omar and Leila raved about the various attractions awaiting us in their home town. I was looking forward to exploring the ancient city of Istanbul, but I was much *more* interested in exploring what other secrets Leila might be hiding. If her expert massage of my private areas was any indication, I expected her to be quite a minx when she was freed from her father's oversight. But I also knew it would be difficult for me to wait the remaining four days for our train to reach its final destination before I could have more of her. While Omar graciously offered to pay for our meal and thanked the waiter for his excellent service, I quietly slipped a note under Leila's napkin with my room number.

With any luck, she'd be able to find some time to slip away later in the evening to join me in my private boudoir.

4

After dinner, the four of us returned to our individual staterooms to catch up on email and change out of our formal wear. By now, the train had reached the Swiss border, and I looked out the window peering up the soaring Alps. The juxtaposition of the lush green valleys and the snow-covered mountains provided a calming culmination to my exciting first day on the Orient Express, and I soon fell asleep from the soft rumbling of the train as it sliced its way through the deep canyons.

I awoke a few hours later to a soft tap on my door, and I threw on the plush terrycloth robe hanging in the bathroom while I approached the cabin door warily. In my still-groggy stupor, I'd temporarily forgotten about the note I left for Leila in the dining car, but when I saw her through the peephole, my pussy throbbed in excitement. I opened the door and noticed that she'd changed into skinny jeans and a tight t-shirt that hugged every inch of her curvy body.

"Leila," I said, peering into the hall to make sure she was alone. "I wasn't sure if you got my message..."

"I had to wait a few hours for my father to settle into his stateroom." she said. "I think maybe he has a visitor, so I've got a little time while he's distracted–"

"Come in," I said, practically yanking her out of the hallway into my bedroom. "*God*, you look so sexy. I haven't been able to stop thinking about you all day."

Without saying a word, Leila placed her thumbs under the bottom of my belt and pulled it apart, dropping my robe to the floor. For a moment, I stood stark naked in front of her, shocked at the boldness of her action for someone her age.

"Something tells me this isn't the first time you've done something like this," I panted, feeling my nipples hardening as she admired my yoga-studio-toned body.

"It's the first time I've done this with a *woman*," she said, running her hands softly around the sides of my heaving breasts.

"Not counting earlier today," I smiled.

"Right, but that hardly counts. It was far too quick and one-sided. I've been wanting to fuck you ever since I watched you touching yourself in the bar car."

"Let's get you out of those clothes," I said, pulling her toward the bed. "This time I want to touch *every* part of your magnificent body."

The two of us flopped down on top of the mattress while we unbuttoned and tugged off her clothes, until she lay nude beside me. We pulled each other close and intertwined our legs as we pressed our breasts together, kissing passionately.

"*Damn*, girl," I panted. "You sure don't act like a schoolgirl."

"No?" she said, gazing at me coyly. "How exactly are schoolgirls my age *supposed* to act?"

"Like *this*," I said, flipping her onto her back and leaning over her while I grabbed her firm tits in my palms and suckled her erect teats like a hungry calf.

"No fair," she panted, arching her back as I threaded my thigh between her legs toward her steaming pussy. "It's my turn to lick *you* this time."

"You'll have your chance soon enough," I said, placing my palm over her crotch and plunging two fingers inside her wet tunnel. "Right now, I just want to *look* at you while I caress you all over."

As I finger-fucked her with my hand, she squirmed on the bed and peered up at me with parted lips.

"Do you *like* that?" I taunted her. "Do you like being probed while you lie pinned on the mattress, only able to peer back at me?"

"You mean the same way I fucked you with my foot under the table in the restaurant?" she smirked.

"Exactly," I said. "That was very rude of you. You put me in an uncomfortable position sitting right next to your father."

"You didn't seem to mind it too much at the time. Besides, he seemed preoccupied with your lady friend. He had no clue what I was doing to you under the table."

"You're a very naughty girl," I said, pushing her over onto her side while I spread her legs into a scissor position. "Now it's my turn to have my way with *you*. I'm going to fuck your sweet pussy and watch you whimper and moan the same way you did with me."

I raised myself up into a kneeling position and straddled her thighs, pushing my pussy toward hers, then I tilted my hips until our vulvas merged, rocking my wet lips against hers. Leila groaned softly, reaching up to squeeze my tits, but I extended her upper leg and swung it between my breasts, pulling her harder against me.

"*Fuck* yes," Leila hissed, throwing her head back against the mattress. "Fuck my cunt with your wet pussy, Jade. That feels so good."

"Better than my *head* between your legs?" I smiled, humping her more vigorously.

"Yes," she grunted. "At least this time I can *see* what you're doing to me."

"That works *both* ways, young lady. I far prefer looking at your pretty face than having your tartan skirt pulled over my head."

"Oh?" she smirked. "You didn't enjoy eating out the innocent schoolgirl in the private lavatory?"

"Not as much as I did sucking on my lambchops while you fucked me with your foot under the table in full view of all the other restaurant patrons."

"You seem to have a predilection for dangerous public sex," she smiled.

"Maybe," I said. "But I also like having you all to myself, where I can live out *all* my fantasies in the privacy of my own bedroom."

"You better hurry up then," Leila panted, digging her nails into the side of my hips as our pussies slurped loudly over the background rumble of the train. "Before my father looks in on me and sees that I've disappeared from my cabin."

"Yes, baby," I groaned. "I'm going to cum all over your sweet pussy while I imagine all the dirty things I want to do to you. Come with me while I grind my cunt against yours."

"Yes, Jade," Leila panted. "I'm close. Fuck me harder. Let me feel your tits caressing my leg while I gush all over your twat."

"Holy *fuck*," I screamed, suddenly overcome with passion at her dirty talk and the look of pleasure on her face as her mouth widened approaching her climax. Suddenly, her body jerked violently, and I felt a gush of fluid spraying all over the inside of my thighs as a crimson flush spread over her upper chest and face.

"Oh God, Leila," I hissed. "I'm cumming baby. I'm cumming all over your sweet, slippery pussy."

While I wrapped both of my arms around her leg, now pointing straight up in the air between my bouncing tits, I felt my pussy clamp down hard as I emitted hard jets of my own all over her pulsing hole. Between the two of us, our juices were spraying in every direction, and I blinked as it squirted all the way up into my eyes. But I hardly cared, reveling in the sensation of our commingled love juices running down over the front of my face while she stared up at me.

After we both finished coming hard, I collapsed onto the bed beside Leila and we giggled as we spread our lubrication all over our breasts and stomachs.

"That was *insane!*" Leila panted, rolling over to kiss me. "Who knew having sex with a *woman* could be so much fun?"

"And *sticky!*" I said, rolling her nipples softly between my slippery fingers.

"I thought *I* was the only one who squirted like that," she said.

"So did I," I smiled. "You're the first one I've been with who could do it with me at the same time."

"What other firsts can you teach me before my daddy catches me breaking curfew?" Leila asked.

"Well," I said, reaching into my nightstand for the double-sided dildo I'd packed hoping for a moment precisely like this. "Have you ever tried one of *these*?"

"Not one as long and flexible as that one," she said, peering up at the silicone dildo as I shook it in the air. "Is that what I *think* it is?"

"That depends what you think it is," I smiled. "You can use this thing in so many interesting ways."

"*Show* me," Leila purred. "I think it's about time one of us got fucked with something bigger than a finger or a toe."

"I thought you'd never ask," I said. "Assume the position."

"Which position did you have in mind?" she grinned. "I mean, it looks like you could fuck me with that thing in all manner of positions."

"That's true," I nodded. "I've tried it with both of us on our backs, on our knees ass-to-ass, and even in the pile-driver position. But this time, I want to be close to you while we enjoy it together. Let's sit facing each other on the bed while we kiss and hold hands. It might be fun to watch each other while we're both humping this thing."

"You seem to have a lot of experience trying different things with women," Leila said.

"It wasn't always this way," I said. "But once you decide to go *femme*, you quickly learn there's no longer any need for men."

"Ha, ha," Leila chuckled. "Especially when we have our choice of giant phalluses. I'm in–fill me up with that thing. This time I'm going to watch you squirt all over my pussy while we come together."

"You're way ahead of me, girl," I smiled, positioning my hips in front of hers and spreading my knees apart as I inserted one end of the long dildo into Leila's box before pressing my hips forward and thrusting the other end in my hole while we clasped hands and moaned feeling the instrument filling us both up.

"Uhnn," Leila groaned, watching the pink appendage disappear into our slits as we began to rock our hips together, gazing excitedly into each other's eyes. It didn't take long for the sight and sensation of the double-sided dildo plowing in and out of our flapping pussies to have the desired effect, and within minutes we were both moaning and squirming on the bed, squeezing our hands tightly together as both of our mouths parted and we stared into each other's eyes nearing another mutual climax. When we both tipped over the edge, our eyes darted down between our legs, where we watched with joyful celebration as our pussies squirted powerful streams of lubrication over each other's stomachs.

It seemed to take forever for the two of us to stop cumming, but when our orgasms finally began to subside, we flopped down on the bed in opposite directions, peering outside the picture window at the snow-capped mountains passing by.

"Talk about a *peak experience*," Leila panted.

"You got *that* right, girl," I moaned contentedly.

Suddenly, we heard a loud tap on the cabin door and we both jerked upright, looking at each other with frightened eyes.

"You don't think that's–" Leila shuddered.

"Let's hope not," I said, thinking the same thing. "Why don't you lock yourself in the washroom just in case, while I check out who it is. Don't worry, if it's your father, I'll tell him I haven't seen you since dinner."

"Thanks," Leila said, scurrying into the washroom and closing the door behind her.

I straightened my hair, then pulled on my robe and approached the door cautiously. When I looked out the peephole, I was relieved to see Adele peering back at me. I opened the door a crack, not wanting her to invade Leila's privacy, and placed my face against the opening.

"Adele!" I said, pretending to be surprised. "What brings you back this way so late at night?"

"I was hoping you might be interested in picking up where we left off earlier in the day," she said. "I've been thinking about you ever since we shared that intimate moment together in the bar car."

"I've been thinking the same thing," I said. "But it's getting late and I'm kind of tired–"

"Who are you kidding?" she said, forcing my door open. "This room *reeks* of sex. Something tells me you haven't been alone in here all this time..."

"I don't know what you mean–" I protested, trying to block her ingress.

She took one look at my messy bed and smiled back at me.

"Just as I thought," she smiled. "You obviously haven't been alone. And by the look of that glistening sex toy on the bed, I suspect you've been mixing it up with that cute Arab girl once again."

"That wouldn't be appropriate..."

"Oh *please*," Adele huffed, barging past me. "Where *is* she? You didn't think I knew what you two were up to over dinner below her father's line of sight?"

"I don't know what you're talking about–"

"With all your moaning and fawning over your spicy curry? Remember, I was sitting right next to you. You practically gave me a charley horse knocking your legs against mine while Leila foot-fucked you under the table."

"Was it that obvious?" I said, resigning myself to the obvious.

"Only to *me*, apparently. Her father was too busy gaping at my tight bosom and trying to negotiate more favorable banking terms to realize what the two of you were doing right under his nose."

"Thanks for that," I sighed. "But I'm not sure Leila's quite ready to bring another partner into the picture just yet..."

Suddenly, the bathroom door parted open and Leila stuck her head out, peering at us with wide eyes.

"I *knew* it!" Adele said. "The *least* you guys can do is share in the spoils, since I've been the one keeping her dad occupied while the two of you were getting your groove on in here."

"So it was *you* who was in the room with him this evening," Leila said, stepping out from behind the door completely naked.

"I saw Jade passing the note to you over dinner and figured the two of you would be looking for some more quiet time together," Adele nodded. "I just hoped to get in on the fun while your father thinks you're still resting in your cabin."

"What do you say, Leila?" I said, peering at her with a coy smile. "Do you think you've got enough time for a little more girl-on-girl action?"

Leila paused for a moment appraising Adele's sexy body, still clad in her clingy lace dress.

"The more the merrier," she smiled. "Now that I've got a taste for women, I want to sample *all* the offerings before this trip is over."

"Come try a little *French* cuisine then," Adele said, clasping Leila's hand and leading her over to the ruffled bed.

I stuck my head outside the door to make sure no one else was spying, then I closed it softly behind me.

This luxury train ride was turning out to have a lot more extra amenities than I could have wished for. As I plopped down on the bed next to the two women, we all intertwined our legs and moaned as we began caressing and disrobing our new partner-in-crime.

W*ant more all-girl erotic chills and thrills? Download the next volume in the discounted collection:*

No boys allowed...

Sneak peek:

Jen leaned forward and took Holly's left breast into her mouth, then turned her head to glance into the camera. I pushed my laptop away from me a few inches so they could see my pussy and hips displayed in front of the screen. As I circled my clit with the tip of my fingers, I squeezed my breast with my other hand and moaned at the sight of Holly's teat in her roommate's mouth...

READ MORE

MORE FROM VICTORIA RUSH:

Choose your next toe-curling fantasy from over thirty-five spicy stories in Jade's Erotic Adventures. Browse the full collection here:

Click to scan your favorites...

FOLLOW VICTORIA RUSH:

Want to keep informed of my latest erotic book releases? Sign up for my newsletter and receive a FREE bonus book:

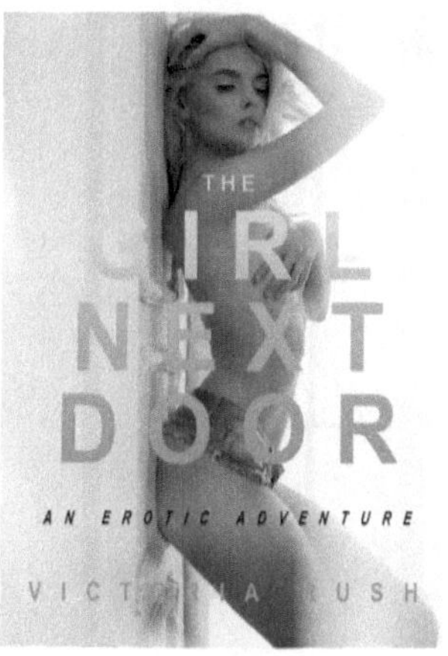

Spying on the neighbors just got a lot more interesting...

www.ingramcontent.com/pod-product-compliance
Lightning Source LLC
Chambersburg PA
CBHW030820210726
48290CB00002B/683